The Island of Mystics

Children of Colonodona Series
Book Two

By
Alisse Lee Goldenberg

pandamoon
publishing

www.pandamoonpublishing.com

Jacket design and illustrations © Pandamoon Publishing
Art Direction by Don Kramer: Pandamoon Publishing
Editing by Zara Kramer, Rachel Schoenbauer, Jessica Reino: Pandamoon Publishing

Pandamoon Publishing and the portrayal of a panda and a moon are registered trademarks of Pandamoon Publishing.

Edition: 1, version 1.01 2019

ISBN-13: 978-1-950627-09-7

Dedication

For my children and all their wonderful aunties. Thank you for all your love and support.

The Island of Mystics

Prologue

She stood on the shore and watched the waves. Her sea-green eyes tracked the horizon, looking for what? She did not know. The cry of her child back at home drove her here to this spot, and her heart ached. Mermaids swam in the wake, their multi-hued heads dotting the surf like jewels in the setting sun. Normally, she would smile at the sight, but now she felt a chill gripping her heart. She turned back to the village. One of her hands slowly rose in a futile wave of farewell. She knew he couldn't see it, but her heart hoped he would know that she had gone down to their beach, that she had lingered there; waiting and watching.

Jerusha had talked to her about her sadness. The wise woman had magic, they said. She could help her as she had helped many others, but her words had driven her here, to the beach where she had first laid eyes on him: her love.

The waves lapped at her feet. Her toes sunk in the sand. Her footprints had long faded away. If she turned to look, she wouldn't be able to see the path she had taken to reach that spot. It felt as if everything in her life was as temporary. Things and people came into her life to make a mark and then vanished without a trace. Nothing lasted.

A tear slipped out of the corner of her eye and made its way down her cheek to reach the corner of her mouth. She tasted the salt of it and thought of the ocean. She stifled a sob as the finality of it all hit her. She loved him. She loved their life, their child. She wanted him at her side, and yet... The wind around her blew hard and moaned through the rocks, giving voice to her silent grief. The first few drops of rain hit the beach as the mermaids in the surf disappeared from view. She shivered as the air grew cold around her. Her eyes hardened as she reached a decision. She no longer cared what everyone else said. Damn their judgements and proclamations. Since her daughter's birth, she saw only emptiness in the world around her. They all said she would see the light once more, eventually. The people in her village; the physicians, the wise ones, all promised an end to the sorrow. And so, they left her to suffer. But no more. She would end her suffering and her pain. It was better this way. She was nothing but a misery to them all. Her own child wouldn't stop crying when she held her, and her husband looked at her in pity. He was better off on his own.

She thought of her precious girl with her turquoise hair, so like her own. Her eyes filled with curiosity, and she felt shackled to her. Her tears were never soothed by her mother's arms. She was a failure. Jerusha was right. To solve the problem, she needed to be taken out of the equation. Marcus would be far better off, raising their daughter alone. Without her.

She walked the beach filling her pockets with rocks. It made sense to do this here. This was where she had found happiness in the arms of her husband. Here was where she would find peace as well. Heart pounding, pockets full, she turned and walked into the waves, letting the sea swallow her grief, as it swallowed her body whole.

Chapter One
Absent Hearts

Audrina sat on the beach. As she looked out over the waves, she sighed. She knew what had prompted this extended vacation to her father's childhood home. Queen Sitnalta and King Navor had both agreed that living among the rubble was not ideal as carpenters and masons worked around the clock to rebuild the burned-out shell of their own home in Colonodona. However, this plan meant that Princess Audrina would have to endure long absences from her best friend and love, Gertrude. Ever since they had both admitted their feelings for one another, the two girls had become inseparable. But now…

Audrina sighed once more. To her right, she could see her brother Lucas wandering along the length of the beach. He too seemed lost to his thoughts. She knew he still mourned the death of his teacher and mentor Kralc, and she knew he also felt a deep responsibility for all that had happened. He now trudged along the sand, not seeming to notice or care that the hem of his cloak was sodden with surf, and was caked with sand. Audrina watched him with pain in her heart. She had been trying so hard to treat him with kindness and a gentleness; to not lash out with annoyance when he pestered her, as she so often used to. She loved her brother dearly, but old habits died hard, and sometimes she felt she slipped up.

She knew that her parents watched their squabbles with bemused acceptance. They knew the love was there; they also knew that siblings were wont to fight with one another. Audrina tried so hard to let Lucas be, to not needle him and she tried to ignore his sullen moods, but he made it so hard for her to do that. He was so mopey and sarcastic around her. Add to the mix her own feelings of listlessness, of being on edge, and her longing to see Gertrude again; it was no surprise that tempers flared between them once in a while.

* * *

Lucas looked out over the water. He could sense his sister's eyes on him and grimaced. Everyone seemed to be walking on eggshells around him. He hated it. He longed for everyone to treat him normally. It had gotten to the point that he was goading his sister into fights with him, just so he could have some sort of outlet. He knew it wasn't fair to her. He noticed that these spats were less intense than they had been in the past, but he relished them all the same. They were bright spots of normalcy in a world where he felt people were treating him as if he were a bruised and broken thing.

He huffed angrily as he looked at the tide rising up around his ankles. He was a dunce, a dupe who had been roped in by a pair of pretty eyes and a kind smile. Lettie had used him as a pawn in her plan for revenge against his parents, and he had fallen for her like an idiot. Because of him, his home lay in a mess of charred ruins, and the wizard Kralc was dead. But he was still here. He was still standing. Lucas just wasn't sure somedays if he deserved it. He saw everyone around him with someone they could lean on and rely on. His parents had each other. Back home, Duke Ipsinki had his wife, the Duchess Gwendolyn. Audrina had Gertrude. Maybe he deserved to be alone? He had once given voice to these thoughts, and his sister had laughed at him and told him not to be so melodramatic. This had sparked one of their fights, and Lucas had felt a flicker of joy at their argument. But this thrill had been cut short by one of their mother's disapproving glares.

The sound of hooves pounding the sand caught the young prince's attention and Lucas looked around to see three men on horseback approaching. He recognized them as his grandfather's men. He waved at them and walked over as they pulled up to a stop.

"My prince," one of the men said with a nod. "You and the princess were expected back at King Parven and Queen Kika's castle some time ago. Your grandparents were starting to worry. We came out to fetch you."

Lucas looked out at the horizon with surprise. The sky was tinged pink. It was clearly far later than he'd realized.

"My apologies," the prince replied. "We lost track of the time. Tell my grandparents we will be back presently."

The men nodded and turned their horses back the way they came. Lucas turned towards his sister and sighed.

"We messed up again," he groaned.

"What happened?" Audrina asked. She saw the dejected set of his shoulders and frowned.

"We were expected back—"

4

"Oh no," Audrina interrupted. She looked out at the setting sun, a sinking feeling in her stomach. "I don't even want to know what time it actually is." She scrambled to her feet and grabbed ahold of her brother's hand. "Let's go!"

The two siblings ran over the dunes, heedless of the sand gathering in the damp folds of their cloaks. They ran together, breathless, and keenly aware of the scolding that waited for them at the castle. Lucas cursed as he realized he'd left his shoes at the beach, certain the tide would wash them away as it came in.

Audrina and Lucas staggered through the castle halls, seeing the disapproving looks of the servants as they took in the prince and princess' bedraggled state.

"What should we do?" Lucas whispered.

"What do you mean?" Audrina hissed back.

"We're so late already. You know that grandfather expects dinner to be on time. Do you think they're waiting for us? Should we change? You know they won't approve of the state we're in."

"If I were you, I would just join us. Never mind cleaning up at this point."

Both Lucas and Audrina nearly jumped out of their skin at the sound of the voice. They turned to see Gerald smiling at them, a merry twinkle in his eye.

"H—how mad are they?" Lucas asked.

"Fairly," Gerald admitted. "But I can't possibly count how many times your mother made Aud and I wait for her as she went on some merry chases of her own." His smile grew wistful as he said Aud's name. "Oh, my queen was forever in a state over Sitnalta. The many times she ate dinner in a dress torn and stained from days playing in a hayloft or climbing trees in the orchards…" he trailed off, appearing misty, lost in a memory. "But you two…I'd say you are both very much like her. Come with me. We'll enter together. It might be safer for you that way."

"Thank you, Grandfather," Audrina said, taking Gerald's arm. With her other hand, she smoothed down her hair as best as she could.

Lucas fell in step beside them. Gerald's words had helped him feel a touch better about things. He gave his sister a small smile, feeling his spirit rise as she smiled back. At least for the moment they were a united front, and he was grateful for it.

Neglecting to change may have been a mistake. Audrina sat shifting uncomfortably in her seat. Her gown was drying and the sand, which was working its way into her underthings was making her itch. She looked up to see Lucas, also squirming in his seat, the discomfort plain in his expression, his purple eyes narrowed in irritation as he attacked the food on his plate.

When they had walked into the dining hall, Audrina had felt a momentary twinge of panic. Her hands had reached up to her blue hair. She knew that in spite of her hasty efforts to fix it, it was still in a state of disarray. She had seen her grandmother, Queen Kika, rake her over with a disapproving look. Her grandfather, King Parven, had a deep furrow between his brows as his eyes had met hers. Audrina had looked over at her parents, expecting to see more disapproval on their faces, and instead, there had been amusement hiding in a stifled smile on King Navor's lips. She could see he'd been trying and failing to appear stern. His brown eyes had sparkled with affection for his children. This had helped quell the nerves fluttering in Audrina's stomach. Her mother had looked at her with bemused annoyance. She had seen Sitnalta look over at Gerald and he had smiled and shrugged as if to say that this was karma for what she had been like as a young princess.

Audrina and Lucas had murmured apologies and had taken their seats across from their parents. She was grateful to have Gerald at her side, providing a genial buffer between herself and the frosty chill emanating off of her grandmother. She had waited for King Parven to begin eating before digging hungrily into her bowl of chowder. It hadn't been as hot as she would have preferred, but she supposed that was her own fault.

The rest of the meal continued in relative silence, with the frigid chill in the air occasionally broken by Navor enquiring into the kingdom's affairs and his father's terse responses.

Audrina and Lucas wolfed down their desserts and after more apologies, the prince and princess were permitted to excuse themselves and retire to their rooms.

* * *

After a long, luxurious soak in her tub, Audrina sat in front of her mirror wearing a dressing gown over her nightdress. Her brush was in her hand, and she frowned as she fought with the snarls peppering her long blue hair. She huffed as the brush caught once more and vowed to her reflection that at the first chance she got, she was going to chop it all off. A knock at the door interrupted her stream of insults at her hair, and she called for whoever it was to enter, more sharply than she normally would.

"Now what has you in such a mood?" Sitnalta asked her daughter as she entered, closing the door behind her.

"It's my wretched hair," Audrina said with a pout. "I hate it. It's hopelessly tangled. I'm going to grab a pair of shears and chop it all off."

Sitnalta smiled at the sullen look on Audrina's face. She remembered all the time she had had this exact conversation with Aud, and the time she had actually done just that.

"What's so funny?" Audrina asked.

"I was merely remembering something," Sitnalta said. She crossed over to the vanity and took the brush. She slowly and methodically began teasing out the knots in Audrina's hair, just as Aud used to do for her, when she had been younger. "I used to say the same thing about my own hair. And one day I did it. I chopped it all off."

"I remember this story," Audrina said. "This was when you escaped from King Supmylo. It was the night you saved Gertrude's father from execution."

"It was," Sitnalta replied. "But, I have to admit that while I cut it off for a disguise, there was a small part of me that was so glad to be rid of it. No more braids, no more knots, no more endless hours of brushing. It was rather freeing."

Audrina giggled. She tried to picture her mother without the long plaits of blue and silver that hung down her back, and she couldn't quite see it. She leaned back into Sitnalta's hands, feeling the gentle tugging of the brush against her scalp soothe her.

"I wouldn't recommend it," Sitnalta said.

"Hmmm?" Audrina murmured. "Recommend what?"

"Cutting it off as I did," Sitnalta replied. "If it comes out like mine, it will look awful. I remember Aud looking absolutely horrified. Or maybe it was because it was the most 'un-princesslike' thing to do." Sitnalta laughed. "I was forever doing things like that. I kept expecting her to give up on me being proper and ladylike. However, if you do want to cut it, we can find someone to do it properly."

Audrina smiled at the suggestion. If it ever came to that, she would take her mother up on her offer. She opened her eyes and caught her mother's gaze in the mirror. "How angry was everyone that we were late?" she asked.

"They were fairly upset," Sitnalta said. "But I think they will get over it. One more apology over breakfast would go a ways to enable that."

"I'll be sure to do that," Audrina said. "And I will be on time."

Sitnalta laughed. "Good idea." She finished her work on her daughter's hair and put down the brush. "But this is not why I actually came to you tonight. I have some news for you."

"Oh?" Audrina turned to properly focus on her mother. "What kind of news?"

"The good kind. By the end of the week, we will be having guests here at the castle."

Audrina's pulse quickened. She tried not to get her hopes up. "Who? Anyone I know?"

Sitnalta's eyes danced with amusement. She saw the expression on her daughter's face. "Oh, no one really. Merely Duke Ipsinki and his family."

Audrina jumped up and hugged her mother tightly. "This is not good news, Mother! This is the best news!" she exclaimed.

"I thought you would be excited," Sitnalta said as she stroked her daughter's hair. "Now get some sleep. I love you, Audrina."

"I love you, too."

Audrina watched her mother go and slid under the covers of her bed. In no time, she was sound asleep, a smile on her face.

Chapter Two
Anticipated Arrivals

Gertrude hung over the railing of the ship. The sea breeze in her face was helping, but she still felt queasy. It had been a miserable week. The weather, once they had left port in Colonodona, had turned violent. She felt as if the sea and ship had conspired against her; tossing and shaking her to the point that she could barely keep water down. She had tried to sequester herself in her cabin, but it had become a stuffy and oppressive prison, only exacerbating her abused stomach. So, Gertrude had taken to cowering on deck, holding onto the railing for dear life, avoiding the piteous glances of the sailors as they passed.

Occasionally, her parents, the Duke Ipsinki and the Duchess Gwendolyn, checked on her; her mother bringing her ginger tea, and murmuring soothing words in her ear, but she tried to keep to herself. Gertrude stood, constantly scanning the horizon, praying to see some sign of land. She had never been out to sea before. Now, she knew that she had no desire to do so again. The main thing keeping her going was the knowledge that she would be seeing Audrina again. They would finally be reunited after what felt like ages.

Hanging over the railing, the sun finally shining, Gertrude smiled, her crooked teeth showing for the first time in days. Her parents had asked her to join them for lunch, but she had declined. Her stomach wasn't behaving as violently as it had been before, and she had no desire of a reprise of the past few days. She heard a squawking sound overhead and, pushing her mousy brown hair out of her eyes, she looked up to see large birds flying above the ship. Their bright, rainbow-hued plumage were like nothing she had seen back home in Colonodona, and she smiled wider in spite of the nausea that clung to her in a nagging persistence. She'd been told that birds were a sign of land. Their voyage was finally coming to a close.

Scanning for the shore, Gertrude's heart fluttered. Soon she and the princess would be together again. Her stomach did a flip, and this time it was not from seasickness. A question, unbidden, reared its ugly head. What did Audrina tell everyone about the two of them? Did her grandparents know? Queen Sitnalta and King Navor were supportive, as were Gertrude's own parents. However, Audrina's letters spoke of how strict and traditional King Parven and Queen Kika were. Gertrude had a nagging feeling that Audrina had kept them in the dark.

"Land ho!" a voice called out.

Gertrude turned to spy a green shoreline appearing on the horizon. From her spot on the ship, she could see spots of colour and more of the rainbow birds. She quashed her worries. Audrina would tell her what was going on. She trusted her. She loved her. Until she knew the situation, she would follow Audrina's lead.

* * *

Audrina stood on the docks, her parents and brother at her side. She was practically bouncing in place, her body thrumming with excitement as she watched the ship drop anchor. She was pulsing with impatience, hoping the sailors would hurry and get everything done and over with so everyone could finally disembark. Gertrude was onboard! Gertrude was such a short distance away at long last. She longed to see her and hold her tight; to speak with her once more, and she soon would be able to do that, if only they would hurry up and lower the gangplank.

The princess watched as the gangplank was lowered and the first passengers finally came ashore. She smiled as Duke Ipsinki rushed forward and kissed her mother's hand in greeting. He then turned and hugged her father. She watched as the Duchess Gwendolyn embraced both of her parents and kissed her cheek. Audrina peered through the crowd looking for one familiar face. She felt the air swoosh out of her in surprise as she was gathered up in someone's arms.

"Audrina!" Gertrude cried. "I made it! I finally made it! I swear, I almost thought I wouldn't. If this voyage has taught me anything, it's that I absolutely detest boats!"

Audrina laughed as she turned and saw Gertrude's crooked smile. Her heart skipped a beat as she took in the girl's quirky beauty. "Oh, Trudy," she said. "I'm sorry your trip was miserable. But I am so happy to see you." All she wanted to do was hold her and kiss her, but she was painfully aware of the crowd that pressed in around them. Not knowing what they would say, she didn't think she wanted to find out just yet.

Gertrude could sense Audrina's indecision, and while she felt the desire to push the issue and pull Audrina closer and show her just how much she missed her, she did not. Instead, she stood back and smiled softly at her, drinking in the princess' long blue hair and soft brown eyes.

"All the misery of the journey was definitely worth it," Gertrude said with a quiet laugh. "I'm here now, aren't I? We're together again."

"That we are," Audrina replied. "I missed you terribly. Come Trudy. Let's go to the carriage. I can't wait to show you everything! It's so beautiful here and I just know you will love it!"

Gertrude's smile widened as she took the princess' outstretched hand. Audrina's excitement was infectious. Though Gertrude was tired from her journey, she couldn't wait for the tour that Audrina was promising.

Leading the way, Audrina took Gertrude to the waiting carriages. She looked back to see if her parents were following with Ipsinki and Gwendolyn, as well as Lucas. Her brother still seemed quiet and withdrawn, as usual, in spite of the smile he had forced out upon greeting his parents' old friends. Audrina frowned and shook her head. This was a happy occasion. She would not let Lucas' moods ruin it for her.

Climbing into one of the carriages together, Audrina and Gertrude sat side by side; hands still firmly lapsed together. Lucas climbed in and took the seat across from them. He offered Gertrude a wan smile and a quiet greeting.

"Hello, Lucas," Gertrude replied. "I missed you. I trust that you are well."

"As well as can be expected," Lucas whispered. He had not slept well in ages, and what sleep he was able to get had been plagued with vicious nightmares. He struggled to pull himself together, not wanting to bring everyone down. He looked up, saw Gertrude's smile falter, and felt a familiar pang of guilt. He had messed up again. "Um, what I meant to say is that I am doing much better now that you and your parents are here with us. It's wonderful to be among friends."

"Of course," Gertrude said. She saw the paleness of the prince's face, and the dark circles under his eyes. "You know, you don't have to pretend around me. As your friend, I care about you and I want you to be happy."

Lucas swallowed hard against the lump that had formed in his throat. He appreciated the sentiment behind Gertrude's words. He just wasn't sure he deserved it. Not sure he could trust himself to speak, he nodded instead.

Audrina watched the exchange and felt something twist inside her. She knew her brother was hurting, and she could understand why. Audrina knew that as his sister, she should be trying to help him. But she didn't know how and felt guilty that she might not have tried her hardest to do so.

"It's the same with me, Lucas,' Audrina said. "I wish you would talk to me. You know you can, right? I—I know it hasn't always seemed that way, but…it's true."

Lucas nodded more vigourously. He felt as if he opened his mouth, he would either scream or cry. It seemed as if everyone around him knew how low he was and it was a disaster. He was so broken, but no matter how good everyone's intentions were, Lucas knew he would never, could never be fixed.

The carriage lurched beneath them as the horses were coaxed into a walk. They started the journey to the castle. Lucas turned away from the two girls across from him under the guise of watching the scenery pass. They stopped speaking to him, and he was glad. He hated that they worried for him. If Gertrude and his sister saw his pain, how must his parents be feeling? He chewed the inside of his cheek as a distraction to keep from crying out at the thought and was rewarded by the coppery tang of blood. They all deserved so much better than to waste their time fretting over him. They would all be better off if he wasn't around.

At that thought, Lucas sat up a little straighter in shock. Why hadn't he thought of that before? Without him no one would worry. Without him they would have peace. It all seemed so simple. He needed to leave and give his family the chance to be truly happy.

Chapter Three
Stealing Away

Gertrude sat and watched the scenery pass them by. Everything was so different from what she was used to back home in Colonodona. The trees here had large fan-like leaves. Many grew bright coloured flowers in vivid reds and oranges. She saw more of the rainbow feathered birds soar overhead. In spite of her fatigue, her eyes remained wide open, drinking in the strangeness and beauty of the island kingdom.

Audrina watched Gertrude staring and gaping at the sights they passed. She couldn't keep the grin off her face at Gertrude's reactions to things. Her enthusiasm and curiosity was infectious. She tightened her grip on the hand in her lap, and her heart skipped a beat at the answering squeeze she received in return.

Soon, they crested a hill and Audrina pointed out the first glance they got of her grandparents' castle. Gertrude's smile widened as she saw the coral-coloured gables, the stained glass windows, and the beautiful pale, rounded towers.

"It's like no building I've seen before," Gertrude said in awe. "It's stunning."

"King Parven would love to hear that," Audrina said.

"Then I'll be sure to tell him."

Gertrude watched as the castle grew larger, the closer they got. Soon she was passing under the marble gateway and being ushered through the doors. She looked around, trying to drink in every detail of her surroundings, the marble floors underfoot, the frescos and flowers that bombarded her sense as she walked by. Everything was new and interesting to her.

"Let me show you to your room," Audrina whispered in her ear.

Gertrude shivered at the sound of her voice and allowed herself to be led down a hall and up a spiralling staircase.

"You're right here," Audrina said opening the door to a large chamber with a light wood fourposter bed.

Gertrude smiled and pulled Audrina through the door and closed it behind them. She pulled the princess close and kissed her. She had been waiting weeks to do that and having her tight in her arms was all she had dreamed of. Gertrude's heart pounded and she felt dizzy with happiness.

When they finally pulled away from each other, both Audrina and Gertrude were breathless. Their faces were flushed, and their eyes were shining.

"I missed you terribly," Audrina said. "I love you, and it has been horrible having you so far away from me."

"I love you, too," Gertrude replied. She stifled a yawn and blushed as Audrina giggled.

"You need to rest," Audrina said. "We'll have plenty of time together now that you're here."

"How can I rest when you are here? All I want is to be with you."

"I promise you I will not leave your side once you have had some sleep." Audrina couldn't stop smiling. Seeing Gertrude and hearing her say she loved her was all she wanted. But she knew how tired Gertrude looked and probably felt after her voyage.

Gertrude watched as Audrina pulled away and started for the door. In an instant, some of the fear she had came back to her. She knew that the princess loved her, but she needed the answer to a question.

"Audrina?"

"Yes, Trudy?" Audrina paused, her hand on the door. She turned back to see Gertrude staring at her with a nervous look on her face.

"Do... do your grandparents know?"

"Know what?" Audrina asked. She knit her brows together, trying to figure out what she was being asked.

"About me?" Gertrude saw the confusion on Audrina's face, and she felt a twinge of nerves.

"They know you're here. They were excited to meet...oh." Audrina realized what she was being asked and she winced. All of a sudden, she felt guilty and tried to figure out what to say. "I...no. I haven't told them about us. I—I mean, it's not that I'm...I know I should have. I mean that I just don't...but I know that..."

"It's okay," Gertrude said with a small smile. "I understand. I just wanted to know... It's that I want to know what I should say or do around them. I know that they are important to you."

"But so are you," Audrina said. "Do you want me to tell them?"

"Only if you do. If you're ready for them to know. I'm not pressuring you."

"I know," Audrina said. "I love you."

"I love you, too," Gertrude replied. "They're your family, and I will respect the fact that they don't know. We're here to see you and your family, and we will have a lovely time."

"Thank you, Trudy," Audrina said. She crossed over and kissed her once more. "I'll see you at dinner."

"Okay." Gertrude watched Audrina leave and sighed. As much as she wished she could be open with her love for the princess, she wouldn't push. Not just yet. She lay down on the bed, ready for some much-needed sleep.

* * *

Lucas looked at the assortment of objects strewn across his bed. His books, letters from Kralc, some clothes, and his dagger were all he needed. Another thought came to him, and he threw a small coin purse into the midst. He grabbed a rucksack and began throwing everything inside. He would go down to dinner and then he would be off. He would go now, but he knew that if he wasn't there for the meal, they would send people after him. King Parven would see to that. For him, meal time was sacred. He thought back to how his grandfather had stubbornly waited for him and his sister the last time they had been absent. He couldn't risk that. He needed to go when he wouldn't be missed.

Certain he had everything he needed, Lucas hefted his pack onto his back and peered out into the hall. It seemed deserted and he took a deep breath. No one was around and he knew he had to act fast. Creeping through the corridors and down the stairwells, Lucas made his way down to the small dock that lay in a little cove at the foot of the castle. There, a small sailboat was moored. Lucas stashed his belongings on board. All he needed now was some food for his journey. That he would take during and after dinner. His pockets would see to that. He would be ready. This would be his final meal with his family, and then they would well be rid of him. This was best for everyone.

Making his way back indoors, Lucas shivered. It would be hard to sit and eat, pretending everything was okay, but he would get through this. He had to. Soon, this nightmare would be over for everyone.

* * *

Audrina sat at the dinner table as the chatter wound its way around her. This was what she had been missing. Her mother animatedly spoke with Gwendolyn about everything that was happening back home, and her father laughed delightedly at a ridiculous joke Ipsinki had told him. Gerald looked on with a twinkle in his eye, and her grandparents seemed to be getting along with their guests. Gertrude sat across from her smiling, and only Lucas seemed to be out of sorts. But this, Audrina had to concede, was usual for him. She resolved to not let this dampen her spirits.

"—and then Micah knocked the thief completely off his feet and he fell into the fishmonger's barrel!" Gwendolyn laughed long and loud as she finished the story. "The other prisoners in the cells complained for days over the smell. Even after he had bathed, the place still reeked of salmon. The guards hated their shifts down there. It was just awful!"

Audrina joined in the laughter. She saw King Parven shake his head in amusement.

"I remember a similar story from the markets here," Parven said to Gwendolyn. "Only it wasn't a fishmonger's barrel. The thief tried to rob one of our taverns. The man who stopped him knocked him face first into a vat of clam chowder. It was horrendous. The stench from his clothes. Everyone swore it was even absorbed into his skin."

Gwendolyn chuckled heartily at this. "I suppose the moral of the story is that thievery is a stinking career choice."

"This is true," Queen Kika added in amusement. "But let us speak of more genteel things."

"Of course," Gwendolyn said. "What did you have in mind?"

"You are well aware of the noble circles in Colonodona. As a duchess, you would know everyone, would you not?" Queen Kika smiled at Gwendolyn kindly.

Sitnalta felt a slight unease at the queen's question. She wondered where she was going with this.

"Well…" Gwendolyn squirmed a bit in her seat. "I am aware of who most of them are. Yes. But I never really ran in those circles before marrying Ipsinki, and now, I still prefer the company of those I help in the villages and the capitol."

"Help?" Queen Kika asked with a quirk of an eyebrow.

"Yes," Gwendolyn said. "Before I was a duchess, I was a hedgewitch. I still am, actually. I do a lot of good work helping people with what ails them, delivering their children, charms, and the like."

"I see," Kika said. "But you are aware of who is around, say, eligible young men?"

"No," Sitnalta snapped. "I see where you're going with this, and we will discuss it later. But know now that she is too young."

"Nonsense," Queen Kika replied with a smile. "It is never too early for a betrothal. My son and you should start thinking about things. My granddaughter will be the queen someday and she should have the right young man at her side. Should she not?"

Sitnalta turned to see Audrina had gone pale. Right young man? She looked to her daughter for how much she should say and saw Audrina shake her head. Not here, not now. Sitnalta nodded to show her daughter that she understood.

Gertrude watched and listened to the whole exchange and felt a familiar sadness wash over her. A betrothal? She knew that things between her and the princess were too good to last. Audrina had a duty to her kingdom. Marriages and unions like the one between Queen Sitnalta and King Navor were rare. Love matches between royalty rarely ever happened, and if Gertrude and Audrina were to stay together, how would they ever bring an heir to the throne into the world? She felt conflicted. She wanted to stay with Audrina forever, but she didn't want to destroy her world because of it. She looked down at her plate and began to push her food around listlessly. She heard the murmur of conversation buzz around her. A soft pressure on her hand pulled her attention away from the mess on her plate. She looked up to see her mother watching her with a soft smile.

"Don't fret, it will all work out," Gwendolyn whispered as she leaned close to her daughter's ear.

Gertrude nodded. She usually trusted her mother implicitly, but with this, she doubted she would be right. She saw only sadness in her future, and she knew that nothing her mother could say or do would change that.

* * *

Lucas wandered down to the dock where his little boat was tied. He turned and looked back up at the castle. He could see lights flickering in many of the windows. Dinner had finished and gone. It had only served to harden his resolve that he was doing the right thing. Watching his parents and grandparents laughing and chatting with one another, seeing them all so happy, he knew that this was for the best.

Footsteps down the path to the dock attracted his attention. Lucas looked up to see Gertrude headed his way. She looked sad and hugged herself tightly as if she were warding away the cold. But the night was balmy and the wind that blew was hot. She wound her way slowly down to where Lucas stood by his boat and watched the waves.

"What are you doing down here?" Gertrude asked.

Lucas shrugged, hoping she would go away so he could make his escape.

"It's a nice night," she said staring out at the horizon.

17

Lucas took a good look at her face in the moonlight and frowned. She looked almost as miserable as he felt. "Are you alright?" he asked.

"Not really," she said.

"What's wrong?" he asked in spite of himself. He wanted her to go, but he also wanted to know she would be okay.

Gertrude sighed. "I guess I'm just realizing that nothing good really lasts. Audrina will be queen someday. I know that our parents support us, but how can we be together if she's meant to rule? I can't force her to choose between me and her duty. It would be unfair. But at the same time, how can I be with her knowing it will just end with the two of us brokenhearted. I just..." she trailed away with a sniff.

"I understand," Lucas said. "It would almost be easier to just up and leave. Staying means watching her be crushed by the idea of letting everyone down, or watching her be with someone who isn't you. Leaving takes the decision out of her hands. It seems the fairest solution."

Gertrude looked at Lucas and at the little boat. For the first time she saw the pack nestled in the craft's bottom, his pockets filled with rolls and scraps. "Is that what you're doing?" she asked. "You're running away?"

Lucas nodded. "I have to," he said.

"But why?"

"It's better for everyone," Lucas said. "The fact that we have no home, that my mother lost Kralc, that our lives are such a disaster, it's all my fault. All everyone does is worry about me. I bring them all down. It would be so much better for them all if I weren't around."

"You lost Kralc, too," Gertrude said softly. "And Audrina was just as fooled by Lettie as you were. If she'd had magic she would have done as you did just as easily. It could have been either of you. That girl was a master manipulator and you know it."

Lucas shrugged. "I don't know."

"I'm not going to change your mind about this. Am I?"

"No," he replied. "My mind is made up."

Gertrude looked at the boat. She sucked her bottom lip into her mouth and chewed on it in thought. "You know your mother will be devastated if you just up and leave," she said after a moment.

"I know she will at first. But in the long run, it will be better for her," Lucas said sadly.

Gertrude watched the prince as he unpacked his pockets into the pack sitting in the boat's bottom. She had a thought and prayed it wasn't a bad one. "Take me with you," she said.

"What?" Lucas replied looking up at her in surprise.

"You're right," Gertrude said. "Everything you said about me and Audrina was right. She needs me gone to make the best decision for herself. I can't be there clouding her judgement, and I can't handle watching her be with someone else, not knowing her heart the way I do. It would be torture. If I love her, I have to leave her." A tear slipped out as she spoke. Part of her truly believed what she said.

Lucas watched her speak. Her voice, her eyes, her body language spoke to her pain. He saw so much of what he felt in her and he nodded. "Okay," he said. "But you have to leave now."

"Can I go and fetch some belongings?" Gertrude asked.

"No," Lucas said. Part of him couldn't trust that she wouldn't alert his parents to his plans.

"Okay," she said after some thought, and climbed gingerly into the boat. She watched as Lucas cast off and began steering them away from the cove and out to see. Within seconds she was reminded of how she hated being on the water but tamped the feelings down. Whenever they docked, she would get word back to the castle and let them know where they were. The prince would be returned home.

Chapter Four
A Perfect Storm

Lucas steered their boat with a sure hand while Gertrude huddled for warmth under a borrowed cloak. She felt badly that she wasn't being more help. Truth be told, she wasn't being *any* help. She wished she knew something about boats so that she could help Lucas sail them away, or at least be some proper company, but her ignorance about boats coupled with her horrific seasickness made her a poor companion on this journey.

"I'm so sorry, Lucas," she said in a weak voice.

"What for?" Lucas asked as he sailed through the waves.

"I'm not exactly pleasant to be around right now," Gertrude said. Her stomach heaved and she bundled herself deeper into the folds of the cloak.

"Are either of us really pleasant to be around at the moment?" Lucas said with a sardonic smirk.

"I suppose not," Gertrude conceded.

"You'll feel better when we make land," Lucas assured her.

"I don't suppose you could magic me a cure for my stomach? Or maybe a pair of sea legs?" Gertrude feebly asked.

"Heh, with our luck, a pair of sea legs would conjure up a pair of legs for you that was actually made of water," Lucas retorted.

"Then never mind," Gertrude said. She offered Lucas a smile. "I'll just leave things be."

"Sounds fair," Lucas replied. "Maybe you should just wait it out. Try and get some rest. I can handle this for the time being. Alright?"

"Thank you, Lucas," Gertrude replied. "I do appreciate that, and I apologize that I'm such terrible company right now." At his nod, Gertrude turned away and tried to focus on taking deep and slow breaths, the softness of the cloak, and what she knew she had to do whenever their journey reached its conclusion.

* * *

Audrina knew that the discussion that had occurred over dinner had not gone over well with Gertrude. She felt horrible about that, but she also knew that whatever she could have said to her grandparents was not dinner appropriate conversation. This was something that she wanted to talk to them about in private. She just hoped that Gertrude understood. She had no intention of marrying any of the noblemen her grandmother approved of. Audrina knew that she had her mother and father firmly on her side. She also knew that Ipsinki and Gwendolyn approved of her and their daughter being together. All she needed was her grandmother and grandfather firmly on their side as well. To know that she had her whole family on her side was a dream for her. She knew that there would be many people who opposed who she loved. And so, she needed her family to be a united front. She had faith that once she explained to them how she felt, and once they saw how she and Gertrude were in love and how perfect they were for one another, they would agree with their son and daughter in-law that this was what was best for the princess.

Audrina made her way towards Gertrude's room and knocked on the door. There was no answer. She knocked again and waited. Still, nothing. Audrina frowned. She had seen how Gertrude had left the table. After the discussion about her potential betrothal, Gertrude had become withdrawn and had barely picked at her dessert. She had left as soon as it was polite to do so, with barely a word to anyone.

"Gertrude?" Audrina called. "Are you okay?"

Her frown deepened as her query still got no response. She turned to see Gwendolyn walking down the hall towards her.

"Princess," Gwendolyn called out as she approached. "Are you alright?"

"I don't know," Audrina said. "I came to speak with Gertrude and she isn't answering the door. I know that the things my grandmother said at dinner bothered her. I just wanted to make sure she's okay. Do you think she could be upset with me?"

Gwendolyn pursed her lips. "I don't think she's upset with *you*. But—"

"But?" Audrina blurted out, cutting her off.

Gwendolyn smiled kindly at the princess. "But, I do think she was upset by the topic your grandmother deemed appropriate dinner conversation. I think you can understand why." She held up a hand to stop Audrina who had opened her mouth to break in. "I know why you didn't say anything at dinner. I understand. These things aren't easy. You know, Micah didn't say anything to King Gerald for years. I also know that Gertrude understands. I think that if she is upset, then it's not at you. It's at the situation. Okay?"

Audrina nodded. "I know. I just wish I could speak with her. Do you think maybe you—?"

Gwendolyn nodded. "I'll go in and see her. Just give me a moment."

Audrina waited as Gwendolyn knocked. She waited and even though no one answered, she opened the door and went inside. In a moment, Gwendolyn came back out.

"She's not there," Gwendolyn said.

"She's not?" Audrina asked. "Where could she be?"

"I don't know. But if I know my daughter, she's probably out walking around trying to clear her head. She needs some time to figure things out." Gwendolyn reached out and placed a hand on Audrina's shoulder. "Just give her some space. She'll talk to you when she's ready. She'll probably talk to you in the morning. Let her sleep this off. She had a hard voyage here, and yes, dinner was not a good experience. Let her get some much needed rest. When she comes back tonight, she'll sleep, and everything will look better in the morning."

"Are you sure?" Audrina asked.

"I am." Gwendolyn steered Audrina away from Gertrude's room. "You know, Ipsinki and I had a hard time during our relationship as well."

"You did?"

"We did," Gwendolyn assured her. "I didn't even want to get married, and I was pregnant at the time with Gertrude."

"You didn't want to marry Duke Ipsinki?" Audrina asked incredulously. In her mind, the duke and duchess were perfect for one another. She couldn't see them any way but together.

"You know, there are other ways of being in love. You don't necessarily have to be married," Gwendolyn pointed out.

"It's just that everyone I know gets married. It's so hard to see a future in any other way."

"Your mother was just the same," Gwendolyn said with a laugh.

"I'm sure," Audrina said.

"Give Gertrude her space tonight. Talk to her in the morning," Gwendolyn said.

"Okay," Audrina said. "I can do that."

"Things always look better after a good night's sleep."

"I'll remember that," Audrina replied.

* * *

Gertrude didn't know when she had fallen asleep, only that she did so fitfully. But when she was awakened for good, it was with a lurching jolt that sent her bending over the side of the boat, sending her feeble remains of her last meal to join the salt spray beneath her. She groaned and looked up to see Lucas surveying the sky, a tension in his shoulders that hadn't been there the night before.

"What's going on?" she asked.

Lucas responded by pointing upwards. Gertrude followed his finger to see the sky black with threatening clouds. A fat drop of rain landed on her face and she heard the distant, ominous rumble of thunder.

"Can you do anything about it?" Gertrude asked.

"If the storm ends up being as big as those clouds make it look, I can't," Lucas said. He went over his options in his mind. His education with Kralc had been left so unfinished. He had gone through his mentor's books and writings, but his sessions doing that had always left him with an ache in his heart, so he did it sporadically and in short bursts. Now he saw how adrift he was.

"Okay," Gertrude said. She'd expected a negative answer and grit her teeth against what she knew was in store for them.

Lucas turned away from his perusal of the inclement weather and turned to Gertrude. He could see how miserable and scared she looked. It had been a mistake allowing her to come along. He sighed and scrubbed a weary hand over his face. Once more, he had failed and someone he cared about was in danger. He briefly wondered if he could use his magic to spirit her away to safety, but as tired as he was he knew he would botch the spell. Even at his best, he knew that anywhere safe would be too far for him to send her.

Gertrude watched him and her frown deepened. "I know what you're thinking, Lucas," she said. "As much as I hate boats, I do not regret coming with you. I can push through this. Let me help you. I'm willing to bet that it will take the two of us to get through this storm. Will you accept my help?"

Lucas heard the wisdom in her words, and he saw the sense in them. He grit his teeth and nodded. "Try and get up to get to me."

Gertrude struggled to her feet, swallowing back the bile that crept to her throat with every movement. She slowly made her way to where Lucas was standing, leaving the cloak behind so her movements would go unhindered. "Tell me what to do," she said.

"Before things get bad, I need to show you a couple of things. My father taught me how to sail, and I think I can teach you a bit before the chaos hits." He showed her the rope in his hand. "I'm going to keep this simple. With this, I'm controlling the sail." He gestured to the wooden stick in his hand. "With this, I'm controlling the rudder. The rudder steers the boat. I will ask you to control the rudder. The sail is harder to control and I'll work with that. However, I need you to heed one instruction."

Gertrude nodded. The winds were picking up around them and she could see the strain in Lucas' arm where he kept the sail in position.

"If I tell you to duck, you need to do it. The wind could blow the sail around in spite of my efforts to keep it where it needs to be. Especially in a storm, and I am not that skilled at this. I don't want you to get hurt and the sail could swing around and hit you."

"I will do as you say," Gertrude said. She crept over to where she would be closest to the rudder. She nestled in and took hold of the smooth wooden post that controlled its steering. She could do this, she told herself. This would be fine. She could listen, and everything would work out. As the winds picked up further and another thunderclap sounded the rain began to fall. *What could go wrong?* She asked herself. *Probably everything.* She replied.

* * *

Audrina woke up and rolled over in bed. The morning sun shone through her window and she sat up, letting her covers slide off of her body. In spite of Gwendolyn's words the night before, she had not slept well. She had tried to rest, but it had been fitful at best. She had followed the duchess' advice and had waited, and now she would see Gertrude and they would talk things over. Everything would be fine once she spoke to Trudy. It would work out and they would be happy once more.

Audrina dressed as quickly as she could and raced down the hallways until she got to Gertrude's room. She knocked and waited. No one answered. Audrina frowned. There was the possibility that Gertrude had already gone down to breakfast, but after her long journey, and the way things had been left, Audrina had expected her to sleep a little later. She knocked again, and after she still received no response, she went against her better judgement and opened the door.

Inside, Audrina's frown deepened. The bed didn't look as if it had been slept in at all. Audrina knew that Gertrude preferred things neat and tidy, but she wasn't this exact. The bed looked as if the castle servants had turned it down in preparation for someone sleeping there. Gertrude's night clothes were laid out for someone to arrive and slip into them. Something was very wrong here. Audrina's stomach dropped at the thought that Gertrude hadn't slept there at all. Where could she be?

The princess headed down to the dining hall. It was possible that she was worrying over nothing. It was possible that Gertrude had gone exploring the night before and had maybe fallen asleep curled up in a chair somewhere. She herself had done this on multiple occasions; falling asleep in an armchair after reading a good book for hours. It was not outside the realm of possibilities. But somehow she doubted that was what had happened. Approaching the doors to the room, Audrina hesitated. Hopefully she would enter and see Gertrude at the table with a hot cup of tea, and she could have a good laugh at her worries over nothing. With a deep breath, she opened the door and entered.

Swallowing her disappointment at finding Gertrude absent, Audrina walked around the table and kissed her grandparents, Gerald, and her mother and father good morning before taking a seat at her father's right.

"Did you see your brother on your way down?" Sitnalta asked.

"No, I didn't."

"Hmm…" Sitnalta pursed her lips. "He hasn't been himself. I'm worried about him."

"Well, he probably misses his home," Queen Kika offered. "You all have been through some things. It is to be expected that he's a little upset right now."

"I suppose," Sitnalta replied.

"I have noticed," Audrina said. "Gertrude and I talked to him on the way up from the docks the other day. He knows he can speak with us. I hope he does." And as she said it, she realized she meant it. As annoying as he was, she loved him and he was her family. Thinking back on the trip up to the castle from the docks, she remembered how Gertrude had initiated the talk with Lucas. Gertrude had been upset by his sullen mood. It was possible that wherever Gertrude was, she was with the prince having a chat. The thought cheered her somewhat.

Audrina looked up as Gwendolyn entered with Ipsinki. Greetings were exchanged as they took their seats.

"So, we're waiting for the lady Gertrude and Prince Lucas," King Parven said as he glanced around the table.

"I don't think we should wait," Ipsinki said. "At least, not for our daughter. The voyage here was quite hard on her, and I'm sure she would like the extra rest. If that is alright with everyone."

"I agree with Ipsinki," Navor added. "We just discussed Lucas, and if he's resting, I'm sure it's much needed. If that's alright with you, Father."

King Parven looked at his son and nodded. "I do prefer having everyone here at once. But I also accept that exceptions can be made as needed." He turned and called one of his servants over. The king directed him to bring in the food, and soon everyone was tucking in and filling their plates.

Audrina put on a show of eating along with everyone, but she knew that her mother saw that she took far less then she usually did at breakfast time. Audrina let everyone around her speak and make plans for the day, and soon the dishes were cleared and people began to leave. Audrina crossed over to where Gwendolyn was walking with Sitnalta and stopped them.

"Mother, Gwendolyn, I went to get Gertrude this morning so we could speak before breakfast."

"I know that last night's dinner discussion was not what you wanted to hear from your grandmother," Sitnalta said.

"No, it was not. Not for either of us," Audrina said.

"I think a talk needs to be had with her, and soon," Sitnalta said.

Audrina squirmed. She knew her mother was right. If betrothal talk were already on the queen's mind, she needed to make herself known, at least if she wanted to avoid an engagement to a man she did not love.

"You're right, but that's not why I stopped the two of you," Audrina said. "I did it because I'm worried."

"About?" Gwendolyn asked.

"About Gertrude. I went by her room and she didn't answer the door," Audrina said. "I went in to see her, and her bed hadn't been slept in. I don't think she went up there at all last night. I don't know where she is."

Gwendolyn knit her eyebrows and frowned. This was unlike her daughter. She wondered where she had gone. "Do you have any ideas?" she asked the princess.

"The only thing I can think of is that she might be with Lucas. Or that she went exploring last night and fell asleep elsewhere. Mother, do you know if my brother went to bed last night?"

Sitnalta shook her head. "I didn't check. I can go and do that."

"Please do," Gwendolyn said. "I will go and tell Ipsinki what you said, Audrina, and we'll start searching for her. It's not like her to just start exploring someone's home without their permission, or without someone with her. It seems strange."

"It does," Audrina agreed. "That's why I came to speak with you."

"I appreciate that." She turned and saw her husband and Navor having an animated conversation about boats. She gestured for them to come over and turned to Audrina. "We'll find her. Don't worry."

Audrina nodded, but she couldn't shake a sinking feeling that the trouble had only just begun.

* * *

Wind and waves buffeted the small boat as Lucas and Gertrude struggled to stay afloat. The storm had started and was attacking them with a vengeance. They had screamed themselves hoarse in order to be heard over the noise of the squall. Gertrude felt as if they were fighting a losing battle. Lucas had managed to cast a shielding spell over the two of them, and it had managed to keep the worst of the rain off of them, but they still shivered in the cold and the wet of the storm. The boat threatened to capsize, and Lucas quickly focused his energy on casting a spell to magically right themselves. Sweat beaded his brow, mingling with the rain that soaked his hair. His pulse pounded in his chest and temples. He didn't know how much longer he could keep this up. Fatigue was setting in and he felt sick.

Gertrude watched Lucas struggling with growing unease. She wished she had talked Lucas out of his plan to run away, rather than hopping on board. Her hand slipped on the rudder and the boat jerked to the side, throwing them both off balance. She shouted a hasty apology, wiped her hand somewhat dry on the skirt of her dress, and fought to right their course. Lucas gave Gertrude a curt nod and focused on his work with his spells and the sail.

Lightning ripped through the sky and thunder boomed around them. Gertrude jumped and shuddered at how close it sounded. She chided herself for being silly. In their situation, there was a lot more to fear than the sound of the thunder. She focused on keeping their boat pointed straight ahead. Lucas had planned a course through the waves. They couldn't possibly go perpendicular to them. The high squalls would capsize them in a heartbeat. She didn't know if it was morning or night. The clouds were too dark to see any hint of sun or moonlight.

The wind blew the rain so that it hammered down around them on the boat. It was impossible for Lucas to see if the water that filled the bottom of the boat came from the clouds up above, or the waves they sailed through and crashed down around them. Lucas felt his strength ebbing and knew that it wouldn't be long before it failed him entirely. He looked up above. If Kralc could see him now, he would be horribly disappointed in his former student. He bit back a sob. He had to find some way to stay strong. If not for himself, then for Gertrude. He would not let Ipsinki and Gwendolyn lose their only child. He would not let Audrina lose the woman she loved. He clenched his jaw and focused hard on keeping their sail in position, and on keeping the rain at bay. He peered through the darkness. Up ahead, he thought he saw lights twinkling in the distance. He prayed that it wasn't wishful thinking.

The wind blew harder. The ropes in his hand trembled with the force of the sail blowing hard and straining the slack. Lucas felt the fibres of the rope in his hand burning against his skin as they dragged through his grip. His resolved slipped as his vision swam before his eyes. He knew he couldn't keep it up much longer. He felt the rope slip through his fingers and he lunged to grab it once more, but to no avail. He yelled out a warning to Gertrude, but his voice was hoarse and croaky.

Gertrude saw Lucas stumble forward as the rope he'd been holding. She heard him cry out what she thought was a warning but she couldn't make out the words. She looked up, afraid, and saw the sail swing. She quickly ducked out of the way but reacted a second too late. She felt the force of it, heard the crack as the gunwale struck her hard on the side of the head. The pain radiated through her body as the rudder slipped through her hands. The boat flipped and both Lucas and Gertrude were surrendered to the cold and darkness of the water. Gertrude had a moment of cold and clarity before the dark swallowed her up and she knew no more.

Chapter Five
A Search Party

Audrina felt the tension creeping up her spine. It grew with each drop of rain that pounded against the castle's windows and on the roof. As the day wore on, she, her parents, Ipsinki, and Gwendolyn were engaged in a fruitless search for both Gertrude and Lucas. Her grandparents had recruited the castle's guards to help in the search. The servants were all on high alert, but so far, even with all the manpower they had at their disposal, there wasn't a single sign of either one of them. Audrina wanted to scream. She didn't know where either of them could be.

"They'll turn up," Gerald said as he approached the princess. He tried to offer her a smile, even though he knew that it wouldn't do much good to make her feel better.

"Do you think so?" Audrina asked. She doubted it. Her mood was as bleak as the sky outside.

"I do," he replied. "It's my experience that in these situations, it never does one any good to think negatively. I have to believe that everything will turn out alright it the end."

"Then where could they be?" Audrina asked. "While they were out searching, they discovered that a boat is missing."

"So, maybe they went out for a sail," Gerald suggested.

"In this weather?" Audrina was incredulous. "I highly doubt that. Gertrude had enough trouble with the sea crossing to get here, and the weather wasn't half this bad."

"Fair point," Gerald replied. "Then they have to be somewhere in the kingdom. Perhaps they went to the docks, or sightseeing, and they got waylaid by the storm?"

"I suppose…" Audrina turned away to look out the window. The rain continued to pound against the glass. She hoped that wherever Gertrude and Lucas were, they were warm and dry.

$* * *$

Lucas rolled over and groaned. His lungs burned, his limbs felt as if they were made of jelly. He had sand caked all over the side of his face, weighing down his clothes, and making its way into every crack and crevice of his body. He wrenched his eyes open and winced at the brightness of the light. He took a deep breath and opened them once more. He had to find Gertrude. He had to make sure that she was alright. He pulled himself into a seated position and coughed. His throat felt as if he'd swallowed sandpaper. He needed water, but all he saw was the sea. He wished he had a bed, a hot meal, a drink of water, all things that he did not have. He turned his head. Every movement hurt. A short distance away, he saw Gertrude lying prone on the beach. She wasn't moving. His heart leaped into his throat and he was afraid. Lying all around her was the debris from their boat. None of their belongings were in sight. He knew that they were all long gone. He crawled over to her and rolled her onto her back. Her eyes were closed, and all along the right side of her face was a dark, livid bruise.

"Gertrude!" Lucas called to her. He placed a hand onto her chest and let out a breath in a rush of relief as he felt her heart beating beneath his fingers. He leaned over her and felt a soft breath against his cheek. "Gertrude," he said once more. "Please wake up. Can you please wake up now? Are you okay? Please be okay."

He heard her moan and saw her struggle to open her eyes.

"Gertrude," he said. "It's okay. We're safe. We're on a beach. The boat is destroyed, and I don't know where this beach is. But know where we are is a safe place. At least for now." He knew he was babbling, and he took her hand in. The more he spoke, the more he saw her respond. Her fingers squeezed his in response and he kept speaking. "I'm sure we can find a shelter here. The weather has cleared up and we're safe here. We'll be alright and safe. We don't need a boat because we are here on a lovely sandy beach."

"Lucas?" Gertrude asked. She heard him speaking to her, his voice registering in a panicky staccato. She tried to open her eyes so she could see for herself that he was okay, but the light from the sun shining overhead pierced her skull with a pain like none she'd ever felt before. She whimpered against it and felt Lucas give her hand a tight squeeze.

"You need help," he said. "I can… I can…go find some? No. That will leave you alone. I can't do that. Oh! I don't know what to do!"

"Lucas?" Gertrude whispered. "Please calm down." Her head throbbed with every word she spoke. She didn't think she'd broken anything, and the only thing she was aware of hurting was her head, but she was too afraid to move and find out if this were, in fact, true.

"I'm so sorry," Lucas said. Gertrude was speaking to him. This was a good sign. He decided to believe this meant she would be okay. "What do you think we should do?"

Gertrude tried to think of an answer to his question. She knew they needed a plan, but the very act of thinking was painful to her. She felt a tear squeeze out as she screwed her eyes shut tighter, trying to block out any trace of light. Even the smallest glimpse of it felt like a vicious assault.

"I don't know," Gertrude whispered.

"You're hurting," Lucas said softly. This settled things for him. He needed to find help. He had no idea where they were, if there were even any people around. And if there were, there was no telling if they were friendly. But he had to find out. He gently let go of Gertrude's hand. "I'm going to go for a little bit," he told her. "We need to find help. I will only be gone a short while. I'll be right back to check on you; hopefully with someone who can help us. Okay?"

Gertrude tried to nod and instantly regretted the action. "Okay," she croaked out.

Lucas hesitated. She seemed to be in such pain, he hated leaving her on her own, but he felt it had to be done. "I'll be right back," he said again and turned to go.

He looked around and gasped in shock. A young woman was staring down at him from the top a bluff and she looked just as surprised as he felt.

Chapter Six
The Island

Lucas gaped for a moment at the young woman as she ducked down, out of sight behind the dune. He caught a flash of turquoise hair and her dark complexion. For a moment he was convinced that he had seen a mermaid on the beach, but he shook his head at the thought.

"What's going on?" Gertrude murmured. She had seen the look on his face, and she wanted some answers.

"There's someone here with us!" Lucas answered.

"A friendly someone?" Gertrude asked.

"I hope so. Wait here. I'm going to go find out."

"Be careful," Gertrude whispered. She didn't know if he'd heard her as he gingerly got up and began walking over to where the woman had been.

Lucas cautiously crept over to the dune. He was moving stiffly and he was sure that if she were still there, she heard him coming. He saw no way around the large bank of sand and he doubted he'd be able to climb, the way he felt. Every part of his body felt battered. As he stood there, puzzling things over in his mind, he saw movement out of the corner of his eye and turned to face the young woman who had been watching him earlier. He stood, taking in her appearance, gauging whether she could be friend or foe. She wore her long turquoise hair in three braids that were tied together at her back. Her eyes were a bright cornflower blue, and they watched him with a keen interest. Her dress was short and flowed around her knees. Her feet were bare. Strapped to her waist was a curved bronze dagger. Lucas eyed the dagger warily. She followed his gaze and raised her hands to show him that she had no interest in using it against him. He stepped forward and placed a hand on his own chest.

"My name is Lucas," he said. "My companion and I were shipwrecked in the storm last night. She's been injured and we need help." As he spoke, he realized that there was a chance that she wouldn't understand him. "I'm sorry. I don't know where we are. Do you understand me?"

She smiled. "I do. You are speaking the common tongue. My name is Zayna. If you will permit me, I can go over the dunes. Help for you will not be far. We are a friendly people and have no quarrel with anyone. If you are peaceful with us, and forthcoming, we will be with you. We can help you and your companion, and soon you will be fit for travel once more."

"Thank you," Lucas said. He felt a profound relief at her words. "I appreciate all you can do for us." He watched her nod and scramble up over the dune and out of sight. He waited a moment and ran back to Gertrude. "Help is on its way."

"I heard," she said. She felt sick. The pounding in her head was awful. She hoped that whoever was coming hurried. She didn't know how much longer she could deal with her head feeling as if someone was trying to hammer their way out of her skull.

Lucas reached down and took Gertrude's hand in his. "She saw you. I know it. I said you were hurt, and I think she understood how important it was that she hurry. We'll be okay here."

"Where is here?" Gertrude said. She thought that maybe if he talked to her it would distract her from her pain. "Who was she? I only caught snatches of what was said."

"She never told me where we were," Lucas said, keeping his voice low, so the noise wouldn't hurt her further. "She said her name was Zayna. I think she was nice, but..." his voice trailed away. He didn't know if he trusted his judgement. Lettie had seemed nice too when he had first met her.

"You don't know if it's true," Gertrude said. "Lucas, not everyone is Lettie. Sometimes people are as nice as they seem."

"And sometimes they're not," Lucas replied.

The sound of horses caught Lucas' attention. He turned to see Zayna riding down the beach with a man at her side. He was seated atop a wagon pulled by a large chestnut mare.

"Lucas," Zayna said as she dismounted. "This is my father, Marcus. He is one of our councilmen and a skilled healer."

"How can I possibly thank you?" Lucas said.

"Don't thank us yet," Marcus said, climbing down off his wagon. He walked over to where Gertrude lay and winced in sympathy as he saw the bruising and swelling along the side of her face. He carefully touched it as gently as he could, while still trying to ascertain the extent of her injuries. "Can you move?" he asked her.

"I don't know," Gertrude said, whimpering as his fingers palpated her face. "I—I've been afraid to try."

"Please try," Marcus said. He helped coax her into a seated position. "Okay. Now, I need you to try and get up. Can you do that?"

"I—I'll try," Gertrude gasped. Her vision swam as his strong arms helped pull her up onto her feet. She cried out as she swayed. Her knees buckled under her and she nearly fell back down onto the sand below.

Lucas ran forward as he saw Gertrude sink down in Marcus' arms. "Gertrude!" he said as he helped Marcus keep her upright. Zayna joined him and together the three of them helped Gertrude hobble over to the wagon. Zayna and her father helped Gertrude up and nestled her down into the blankets and pillows they had set up inside.

"I'll try and keep the ride to our village as smooth as possible," Marcus assured her.

"Thank you," Gertrude said.

Lucas was alarmed as he heard how weak her voice sounded. He climbed up in and sat beside her.

"Do you have any belongings that washed up with you?" Zayna asked.

"No," Lucas said. "I only had one pack, and I didn't see it anywhere when we came ashore."

"Okay," Zayna said. She swung up into her horse's saddle as her father climbed up into the driver's seat of the wagon.

She led the way, and as Marcus turned his horse around to follow his daughter, Gertrude reached out and took Lucas' hand in hers as the wagon's swaying exacerbated the pain in her head. Lucas squeezed her hand in reassurance and he looked back at the remains of their boat as they were taken away and into the streets of Zayna's village.

* * *

The day had come and gone, and still there was no sign of either Lucas or Gertrude. Sitnalta stood on the balcony of the castle, overlooking the sea. She leaned against the rail and cried. Her son was nowhere to be found. Her best friend's daughter was also missing. The only comfort she had was the thought that wherever they were, they were together. But she couldn't help thinking that there was a chance that she would never see them again. She might never hold her son in her arms again, or see his smile, hear his laugh. She knew that she was wallowing in morbid thoughts, but she couldn't help herself. A part of her wondered when it would stop. She felt afraid that she would never stop losing those she loved. Najort, Aud, Kralc, now Lucas and Gertrude. Who was next? She wanted to scream out to anyone who might here to please, make it stop. It was unfair.

She turned as footsteps sounded on the balcony behind her. She hastily reached up and tried to wipe away the tears that had run down her cheeks, but stopped when she saw her husband approach. She had no reason to hide her feelings from him.

"I thought I'd find you out here," he said as he came closer. He put his arms around her and held her close.

"I just needed some time alone," she said. "I thought being out here, the sea air might help. It was getting so stuffy in there. But looking out at the water, knowing that there's a boat missing, I can't help wondering…"

"I know," Navor said. "I'm wondering the same thing. Are they out there?"

"The storm was so violent last night," Sitnalta said. "If they were out there. I don't want to think about what could have happened. And yet, my mind can't help go there."

"I understand. But we need to stay positive. For each other, for Audrina, and for Ipsinki and Gwendolyn," he said. He placed a kiss on the crown of her head. "I can't think of anything bad happening to our son. He's a strong boy. We've weathered worse than this. I have to believe that, wherever he is, he's coming home to us. I need you to believe that, too."

Sitnalta looked up into Navor's eyes and saw that he believed his words. But then she remembered how down Lucas had been lately; how sad he'd seemed the last time she'd seen him at supper. "I don't know if I can," she said, as fresh tears slid down her cheeks.

Chapter Seven
The Council's Decree

Audrina walked listlessly through the castle's corridors. Everywhere she turned she expected to see either Lucas or Gertrude, and with every look around the corner she felt an aching disappointment.

Ipsinki came into view and gave the princess a sad smile. "I can see you're feeling it, too," he said.

"I don't understand," Audrina said.

"You're looking for them everywhere. I just don't see what could have happened. It's not like her to run away." He sighed and leaned heavily against the wall.

"Run away?" Audrina asked. "Is that what you think happened?" She felt weird at his words. A shiver ran up her spine.

"I can't see any other possibility," he replied. "There's no evidence they were abducted. No sign that anything worse happened. Apparently, Lucas is missing some belongings. It seems that he, at least, planned to go. I just don't know why my daughter would do this."

Audrina went pale. "I do," she said in a hollow voice. "And I know why Lucas went as well."

Ipsinki saw how sick Audrina looked. She appeared shaken. "What is it?"

"It's me," she said. "This is all my fault."

"What are you talking about?" Ipsinki said with a frown. "How can this be *your* fault?"

"I knew Lucas was upset. He was having such a hard time with everything that had happened back home, with Lettie, Kralc's death, our home burning down... He felt responsible, and I didn't exactly go out of my way to help him." She let out a shuddering sigh. "I could have helped him. I tried to treat him with kindness, but I know I could have done better."

"We were all going through something hard," Ipsinki said. "It does no good to beat yourself up. But what does this have to do with Gertrude?"

"It was the talk my grandmother started during dinner," Audrina said.

"Ah, I see," Ipsinki said. "But my daughter is usually more pragmatic than this. I don't see why one uncomfortable conversation would—"

"I don't know," Audrina said. "It became clear that I hadn't told my grandparents about us. Maybe she thought I was ashamed?"

"Oh, Princess," Ipsinki said with a sad smile. "I know my daughter, and she would never think you were ashamed of her. She knows your love is real."

Audrina nodded. She thought back to Lucas and Gertrude talking in the carriage. "You know, there is another possibility."

"What is that?" Ipsinki asked.

"She saw how low Lucas was feeling," Audrina said. "It could be that she saw him planning on running away and she chose to go with him, maybe to help him?"

"That does sound like something she would do," Ipsinki thoughtfully replied. "If that is the case, then maybe we will hear from them sooner rather than later."

"That does sound more hopeful," Audrina said. She gave Ipsinki a small smile.

"Keep your spirits up," Ipsinki said. He placed a reassuring hand on her shoulder. "We'll get them back. I know it."

Audrina nodded and watched him walk away. Even though she felt a small sliver of hope, she also knew that whatever had happened. she was at least partly responsible.

* * *

Gertrude lay back against the pile of pillows in her bed. Marcus and his daughter had led them through a tangle of hallways until they reached a small bedroom. There, Zayna had helped her into a clean and soft linen nightgown. Marcus had come in once she had been safely ensconced in bed and tucked into a soft quilt. He'd handed her a warm cup of tea that smelled like home. She couldn't count how often she watched her mother brew potions for people to ease their pain. The familiar scent of ginger and feverfew mingled with the memory of helping her mother over a steaming cauldron brought a lump to her throat. Her parents must be so worried by now.

"Are you alright?" Marcus asked. "The herbs in this tea will help ease your pain. There is also something in here to help you rest."

"Thank you," Gertrude said. "It just smells like home. My mother is skilled in the healing arts. I help her when I can. She must be scared, not knowing where I am."

"I understand," Marcus said with a smile. "Drink up and heal. I will tell the council about you and your companion. He has been placed in the room next door. He is also getting some much needed sleep. When you are awake, we will bring you something to eat, and hopefully by then, you will feel well enough to be introduced to those in charge."

"I would like that," Gertrude said. She took a tentative sip of the steaming liquid, trying to determine how hot it was. She found just hot enough to drink and felt it warm her as it slid easily down her throat.

Marcus nodded. "There's a small table beside you for the cup when you've finished. I will check on you soon."

"Thank you, Marcus," she said. She hoped that everyone was as kind as the two who had taken them in. Hopefully they would find a way home soon.

She watched Marcus leave and slowly finished her drink. She placed her cup down on the table Marcus and indicated and lay down in the soft, warm bed, feeling the pain in her head slowly subside. She pulled the covers up to her chin and let herself get carried away into a deep and restful sleep.

Next door, Lucas had just finished relaxing in a hot bath. Marcus had given him an assortment of bath oils that had relaxed his muscles and eased his pains. He'd only been mildly surprised at the motley collection of bruises and abrasions that peppered his body. It was only to be expected at the way the waves had tossed him around until he'd landed on their sandy shore. Once clean, he'd dressed in the nightdress that had been laid out for him and then climbed into a cozy bed and fell gratefully asleep. He'd worry about where they were and what to do once he'd woken once more.

* * *

Zayna stood outside Lucas' door waiting for her father to join her. These strangers intrigued her. She'd lived her whole life on this island, and never before had any strangers landed on their beach. They were a secluded nation, and the council had decreed they remain that way. But now, here was her chance to learn about the outside world. She thought about the way that Lucas' purple eyes had looked deep into hers, as if he too were filled with questions. She longed to ask him everything about where he came from. But she knew that he needed his rest and she would give him that.

Her father emerged from Gertrude's room and nodded to her. "I believe that the girl will heal well. The boy's injuries are minor."

"I'm glad," she said. "His name in Lucas, and his companion is called Gertrude."

"Of course," he said. He turned to walk down the hall to where the council met.

"What do you think they'll say?" Zayna asked as she walked at her father's side.

"The council?"

"Mmhmm."

"I'm unsure," Marcus said. "You know how they feel about the outside world."

"I do," Zayna said. "I just never understood why."

"They have their reasons, and they are valid," Marcus said.

"But that happened generations ago," Zayna argued.

"My daughter, I know you have such a curiosity about the outside world, but it's not a world for us," he argued.

Zayna grumbled to herself. It was an old argument. It had been going on between them since she could speak. She knew that they would never agree. They soon reached the council chamber and she stepped back as her father knocked.

"Enter," called the chief councilman from within.

Marcus took a deep breath and walked into the room. Seated at a long table, six men and five women sat in high-backed chairs.

"Marcus," said the chief. He gave the healer a deferential nod.

"Chief Finn," Marcus said, inclining his head in return.

"I hear that we have visitors to the island," Finn replied. "You know our rule about outsiders."

"I do," Marcus said. "However, you know that when I became the head healer of Coralnoss, I vowed that I would help all those who needed it. I cannot leave two people in need of aid lying on a beach, injured and in pain."

"I understand."

Marcus turned his attention to a handsome middle-aged woman who was seated to Finn's right.

"Thank you, Jerusha," Marcus said.

"The fact remains, that with or without your aid, these people would still be on our island." Jerusha turned to Zayna. "Tell me, Zayna, you spoke with these strangers, did you not?"

"I did, councilwoman," she said.

"Tell me your impression of them," she said.

"I do not believe they mean us harm. They are merely two travellers who got lost in a storm," she said. "The remains of their boat are scattered across our shore."

"They were travelling alone?" Finn said.

"They were," Zayna said.

"I see," Finn replied thoughtfully. "They gave you no impression that they were playing you falsely?"

"I see no reason why they would do that," Zayna said with a frown.

"There is always a reason," Finn said, a dark look on his face.

"There was no evidence they lied to me," Zayna insisted.

"I believe you believe that," Finn said. "What are your thoughts, Marcus?"

Marcus thought over all he'd seen of his guests. "I agree with my daughter. I have no reason to believe that these two people are in any way a threat to us. You can trust me on that. You have my word. I will take full responsibility for all they do here."

"Thank you, Marcus," Finn said. He turned to the others on the council. "As we are responsible for all who live under us, you need to understand that we have to take all these things seriously."

"I do," Marcus said.

"As do I," Zayna said.

Finn nodded to them both. "Then understand that the council needs some time to deliberate. We will talk over our options and we will come to a decision shortly. When our guests wake up, and you determine they are capable of it, bring them before us and we shall make our own decision as to their character. We will take your input into account as well."

"Thank you, Chief Councilman. I appreciate the care you take in your leadership," Marcus said.

"As do I," Zayna said with a small bow in his direction. "I have faith that you will come to the right decision."

"We will," Finn said. "And you need to understand that what is right for the people of this island will always take precedence."

"I do understand that, Chief Councilman. The people of this land chose you and this council to lead. We have faith you will always do what is right," Zayna said.

"Good." Finn gave Zayna a soft smile. "You have a kind heart. It has guided you well so far. Know that sometimes though, it is best to listen to your head."

"Thank you for your advice," Zayna said.

Marcus reached for his daughter's hand. "We shall return when our guests are awake."

"See that you do."

With that declaration, Marcus led his daughter from the room and back down the hall, leaving the council with a decision to make.

* * *

Lucas woke up and stretched out luxuriously under the pile of quilts he'd been left with. His first thought was that Marcus was a miracle worker. Whatever had been in his bath oils had left him feeling well-rested and his muscles loose and pain free. He rolled over and peered out the window of his small room. It was twilight outside. He had slept through the day. Hearing his stomach grumble, Lucas figured he should get out of bed and let someone know he was awake. Swinging his legs over the side of the bed, Lucas stood up and searched through the small cupboard that stood in the corner of the room. He assumed that everything was there for his taking and figured that whatever clothes he should find he should wear. It would not do for him to go exploring wearing only his borrowed nightshirt. Lucas found a pair of cream-coloured linen drawstring pants and a loose fitting shirt. He pulled them on, smiling at the softness of the fabrics. Once clothed, he opened the door of the room and stepped out into the hallway.

He'd been told that Gertrude was in the room next to his and he hesitated outside her door, his arm poised to knock. He paused. If she was still asleep, he didn't want to wake her. He felt so badly about the fact that she'd been injured while accompanying him on his journey. Lucas wanted to apologize, and he also didn't want to make things worse. He looked down at his bare feet and rubbed his toes against the smooth stone floors. Sighing to himself, he made up his mind and knocked softly on the door. Waiting awkwardly outside her room, Lucas heard Gertrude rustling around inside and soon, the door was cracked open.

"Lucas," she said.

Lucas let out his breath in a whoosh of relief. He was glad to see that the swelling along the side of her face had gone down significantly, and though she was bruised, he was happy to see that she was moving easily.

"Gertrude." He smiled at her. "That Marcus appears to be a miracle worker."

Gertrude smiled and tucked a lock of hair behind her ear. "It seems so," she said. "Are you alright?"

"I am," Lucas said. "I see that you're doing much better."

"I am," Gertrude said.

"Gertrude," Lucas began. He looked back at his feet, nervous to meet her eyes. "I—uh—I'm so sorry."

"For what?" Gertrude asked.

"You got hurt," he said. "It's my fault. If you hadn't run away with me, if I hadn't planned to run away in the first place, you'd still be at my grandfather's castle, and not here, bruised and lost."

Gertrude sighed. "Lucas, you can't keep blaming yourself for everything bad that happens. I made up my own mind to come with you. No one forced me to. You didn't kidnap me and throw me onto your boat, did you?"

"No!" Lucas looked horrified at the thought.

"Then how is this your fault?" She smiled kindly at him and laughed as her stomach growled. "I don't know about you, but I'm starving."

Lucas' stomach growled back in response. "Clearly, I am as well." He laughed and looked at Gertrude who was still smiling at him. "Are you sure you're alright?"

"My head is still sore," she admitted, not wanting to lie to the prince. "But it is nowhere near as bad as it was yesterday. At least, I think it was yesterday. I honestly don't know how long I've been asleep."

"Me neither," Lucas said. He looked down the corridor. "Do you know where we can find some food?"

"I'm as in the dark as you on that one," she said. "But, do you think it's wise to just go exploring on our own? Maybe we should remain here and wait for Marcus and his daughter to return for us?"

"Zayna?" Lucas replied. "She seems nice."

Gertrude grinned as she noticed Lucas flush as he said her name. "She does," she said. "And she was pretty, too."

"Was she? Lucas said, looking away. "I—uh—I hadn't noticed."

"Yes, I'm sure you didn't," Gertrude couldn't help teasing the prince. "Interesting fashion here. Don't you think?"

Lucas' blush deepened as he remembered how short her dress had been. "Yes, it seems as if no one likes to wear shoes. There were clothes in the cupboard for me, but no shoes or boots. And yesterday, neither Marcus or Zayna were wearing any."

"Right," Gertrude said with a short laugh. "That's exactly what I was referring to: the lack of footwear."

Lucas smiled. "Now, I don't think we're prisoners here, so I think it should be allowed to go exploring for something to eat," he said.

"Alright," Gertrude said. "I will go with you. Just let me look through my own cupboard. I'd prefer to not go exploring in a nightdress."

"I'll wait for you out here," Lucas said.

"Give me a moment." Gertrude shut the door and turned to the cupboard standing in the corner of her room. She opened the doors and pulled out a pair of soft pants and a shirt that matched those that Lucas was wearing. She pulled off her nightdress and pulled on the clothes. She marvelled at how comfortable it all was. She turned to the mirror in her room and smoothed out her hair. If anything, the voyage had seemed to improve Lucas' mood, and for that, she supposed she should be grateful. Now, all she needed to do was figure out where exactly they were, and find a way to contact their families. Gertrude knew that they had to be terribly worried about them, and in spite of Lucas' assertion that this was for the best for them, she knew that Sitnalta and Navor's hearts would break if they never saw their son again.

Convinced that she looked as good as could be expected, she opened the door to find Lucas still standing there.

"Alright," she said. "Let's go and find something to eat."

"Great!" Lucas said. He turned and picked a direction.

They set off down the corridor, which curved around and around. Gertrude realized that they were walking around a spiral, twisting towards the centre of the building. Here and there, offshoots would go off in different directions. Lucas maintained that they should stick with the corridor they followed, because it would be easier to find their way back to their rooms.

They walked, and on occasion, they saw strangers who stopped and stared at the two of them. Gertrude stared back, equally curious. The colours of hair she witnessed gave her pause. It seemed as if every colour in the rainbow existed here. She saw violet, green, pink, and the odd shade of blue. She found it fascinating. Back home, the only people with hair like this were Queen Sitnalta and Audrina. Thinking of Audrina made Gertrude miss her more, and she tried to push the thoughts away. She would speak to Lucas of this later.

What she saw of the building felt like a much sparser version of King Parven's castle. It lacked the tapestry and the gilded vases and art, but the white stone floors were similar to his marble, and the smooth stone walls were very close in their resemblance. She supposed this was due to the fact that like Lucas' grandparents' kingdom, this island had a similar environment.

Up ahead, Lucas spotted Marcus walking with Zayna. She turned and smiled as she saw him. She turned and pulled on her father's sleeve. The healer looked where his daughter indicated and he too smiled at them. They stopped walking and waited for Lucas and Gertrude to walk over.

"I'm glad to see you two up and about," Marcus said.

"Thank you for the drink you gave me," Gertrude said. "I feel much better."

"And you?" Zayna asked Lucas.

"I am also doing much better," Lucas replied. "Thank you."

"I'm happy to hear that," she said with a smile.

"I hope it's okay that we left our rooms," Gertrude said.

"Of course," Marcus said. "You are our guests, not our prisoners. Although, I had hoped that we'd gotten to you before you'd woke up. That way we could have shown you around for your first look at our land."

"Thank you," Lucas said. "We just woke up and realized that it had been quite some time since we'd eaten."

"Well then, you need to find some food," Zayna said. "I'd love to take you to get some."

"Thank you," said Gertrude, and giggled as her stomach grumbled once more.

"And afterwards," Marcus said. "The council would like to meet you. They have some questions. We are a solitary land, and they would like to know some things about you."

"I understand," Lucas said. "Now about that food."

In no time, Zayna had them sitting at a small table with their plates piled high with fruits, breads, and hard-boiled eggs. She watched as they devoured all they'd been given and was filled with questions about where they'd come from, what they'd been doing before landing on their shores, and whether or not they wanted to go home.

Gertrude eyed their host's long turquoise hair with interest. At first, she thought that this might be due to the island, but again, King Parven's kingdom was quite similar in that regard, and his subjects had hair and eye colouring like those in Colonodona; skewing towards the browns, blonds, blacks, and occasional reds. It was a sea of earth tones, where here it was more like a rainbow, where she and Lucas were the outliers.

"What is it?" Zayna asked.

"Well," Gertrude began. "It's your hair. I'm sorry if this comes out rudely, but your hair is turquoise, and your father's is green. Already, just walking through these halls, I've seen more colours in your people's hair than I've ever seen back home. I don't mean to offend. I'm just curious. And it's so different from what I'm used to."

"Oh, so everyone has brown hair where you come from?" Zayna asked.

"No, but if you look at it, it all seems closely related in a way. We have some yellows, black, red, and brown. And as people age, it can become grey or silver." Gertrude didn't know why, but she chose not to mention Audrina and Sitnalta's blue locks as an exception.

Lucas caught Gertrude's omission, and he cocked an eyebrow at her. He didn't comment, just listened to the conversation. He too had noticed, and he had found it interesting.

"Maybe it's our environment," Zayna suggested. "Maybe our lands are different, so our people are as well."

"Perhaps…" Gertrude trailed off. She needed to ponder this. It was a bit of a mystery to her.

Marcus entered the room and sat at their table. "The council is meeting, and said that as soon as you're ready, they would like to meet you."

"Of course," Lucas said. He polished off what remained on his plate and took a long drink of some juice. He wondered what fruits it had been made from. It tasted like nothing he'd tried before.

Gertrude nodded, her mouth full of food, and she too quickly finished off all she had been given. They both pushed their plates away and rose from the table. A couple of people came forward and collected their dishes.

"Let's go meet your council," Gertrude said.

"Come with me." Marcus turned and led the way out of the room.

* * *

Lucas walked into the council room with Gertrude at his side. They were led in by Marcus and Zayna, and he found himself staring at a long table at which eleven people stared back at him. His gaze was pulled to the centre by an intimidating man with violet and silver hair. His dark eyes seemed to look right through him, and his expression was carefully neutral. There was no way to know what this man was thinking, but Lucas had the instinct that this was the man in charge. In front of him was a glowing red stone. This stone made him feel anxious. He didn't know what it was, but he did not like it.

"Chief Councilman Finn," Marcus said. "I bring you our guests: Lucas and Gertrude."

"Thank you, Marcus," Finn said in a deep voice. He smiled at his guests, though it did not reach his eyes. "I trust that you are well rested after your ordeal."

"We are," Gertrude said. "We thank you for your hospitality as well as the care we have received."

Finn nodded towards her. "I hope you don't mind, but we have some questions for you. I don't know what you have been told about us, but we are a nation of people who like to keep to ourselves. We don't get many guests, and we prefer to keep it that way. Before we tell you our decision about what we will do with you, I wish to know your purpose here."

Lucas gulped. What they were going to do with them? Something about the way this man spoke and looked at them made him nervous, and he didn't like it. There was something here that felt off, and alarm bells were sounding in his mind. He turned to Zayna, and she looked back at him, seemingly unconcerned. He tried to take that as a good sign, but his feet itched to run away from this place, and these people. Instead, he cleared his throat.

"Of course," he said. "We will tell you all we can."

"I assume that we don't have to tell you that it would be for the best if you were truly honest with us," said Jerusha, from her place seated to Finn's right. "This stone is the truth stone. We will know if you lie."

"We will be," Gertrude said. "That stone will not be necessary."

"We shall see," Finn retorted. "Tell me how you came to be here."

Lucas tried to relax. This was something he could do. This was a simple request for him. "Gertrude and I were sailing and we encountered a storm. In spite of our best efforts, the wind and rain became too much for us, and our small boat capsized. We landed on your beach. We weren't trying to come here. It was purely accidental. And, if I may, landing on your shores probably saved our lives."

"I don't remember much of it," Gertrude added. "During the storm, I was struck by the gunwale." She raised a hand and indicated the bruising, evident on her face. "I awoke on your beach."

"I see," Finn said. This much seemed truthful so far. The stone had not reacted to their words. "Where do you come from?"

"We are both natives of the kingdom of Colonodona," Gertrude said.

"However," Lucas broke in. "This was not where our journey here began. We were visiting my grandparents' island kingdom. They are, I believe, south of here."

"You believe?" Finn asked, his eyebrow cocked at Lucas' turn of phrase.

"I confess that I lost my way in the storm," Lucas said. "I was navigating, but the way the waves tossed us about, and the way the wind blew, I may have gotten completely turned around. I'm unsure of where we are. I've seen no map, and there's no way of knowing which direction we'd been sent."

"I understand," said Jerusha. "Now, tell us, what was the purpose of your journey?"

Lucas sucked on his bottom lip. Here was the question he dreaded. He desperately wanted to lie, but at the same time, if they had some way of knowing what was true, he feared the consequences.

Finn saw the boy's discomfort. His suspicions of these 'guests' seemed confirmed as the boy seemed unable to answer this simple question.

"Lucas?" Gertrude softly asked him. She knew why he didn't want to answer but felt that their situation dictated that they be straightforward about everything. "Would you like me to tell them?"

Lucas looked into Gertrude's eyes and saw her concern and compassion. He frowned. Here she was, looking at him the same way his mother did. As if he were broken. He would show her he was stronger than this. "No," he said. He looked up at the council. "I'm sorry," he said. "I'm honestly ashamed at the answer. You see, I was brought up believing that first impressions are important, and here I am about to make you see me rather badly."

"Explain," Finn said.

Lucas sighed. "We were out in the storm because I was running away from home," he said. "Gertrude caught me as I was leaving and she joined me. She has her own reasons for it, but I felt I had no choice. My presence was not good for my family. I felt I was doing what was best for them."

"In what way?" Jerusha asked.

Lucas looked at her. Her warm voice held no judgement, only curiosity. "I made some horrible mistakes. Mistakes that cost me my teacher and mentor. He died because of me. My family lost their home because of me. This is why we were staying with my grandparents. Every time I looked into the eyes of my mother, father, and sister, I saw pity and sadness. And I knew they saw nothing but pain when they looked into mine. It was best for them if I left."

Zayna heard Lucas' words and her heart broke for him. She could see from the set of his shoulders and the sadness on his face that he'd meant every word he'd said. He appeared to believe it. She knew that there had to be more to the story, and she felt the desire to try and help him.

"I see," Finn said. He turned to face Gertrude. "And what were your reasons for accompanying him on this trip?"

Gertrude sighed. She had known this was coming. "Love," she said.

"You love him?" Jerusha asked.

"No!" Gertrude blurted out. She blushed. "I'm sorry. I do, but I love him as if he were my little brother. Nothing more than that. I left for many reasons. I left because I fell in love with someone who had only love for me as a reason to be with me, and a million reasons to stay far away. I needed space and time to clear my head and figure things out. I left with Lucas because I care about him, and I wanted to make sure he was alright. I don't believe he should be alone. And I do not hold

Lucas responsible for what happened to his teacher and his home. I know that no one else does either."

"You two speak of these incidents in abstracts," Finn said when she had finished speaking. "What happened?"

Lucas looked at Gertrude with a panicked expression on his face. She smiled kindly at him.

"Lucas and his sister were both duped by a young woman," Gertrude said. "She played them both for fools. In fact, she nearly convinced everyone she was sincere. She was after a magical object that Lucas' mother had in her possession. Once she had this object, she destroyed Lucas' home in a horrible fire. Lucas' teacher died in the fire. His teacher chose to go in of his own volition to ensure that this object was truly destroyed so no one else could use it for evil."

"Why did this woman want the object?" Jerusha asked.

"Revenge," Lucas said. His voice sounded hollow as he thought about these incidents. "My mother had imprisoned her father. Her father had been a tyrant that had brought about the death of someone my mother had cared for. He was a cruel and vicious man who had committed other atrocities as well. He had tried at one point to kill Gertrude's father as well."

"And yet, it is you who feels responsible?" Finn asked. "I can't see how."

"I was lured in by her beauty and by the fact that she took an interest in me. I was an idiot. And it was I who gave her the object when she asked for it," he said. He looked down at his feet, scared to meet Finn's eyes.

"Many a person has been swayed this way," Jerusha said. "I understand."

Lucas nodded.

"There are a few more questions from the council," Finn said.

Gertrude looked at them. "Ask away," she said.

"What was your purpose in your home land?" asked a wizened old man at Finn's right.

"I don't understand," Gertrude said.

"What did you do? What were you learning to be?" he said to her.

"I was studying the healing arts with my mother," she said. "She is a hedgewitch and helps people when they are ill. She delivers babies and creates charms for those who need aid."

"And you?" the old man asked Lucas.

"I was studying magic with my mentor before he…before he died," Lucas said. "He was a great wizard, and I had hoped to be one as well."

"Alright," Finn said. "Thank you for your honesty. Marcus," he said, turning to the healer. "Kindly take our guests out to the hallway and wait while we finish our deliberations."

Marcus nodded, and he and Zayna escorted Lucas and Gertrude out of the room.

Once the door shut behind them, Lucas let out a breath.

"That was…something," Gertrude said.

"Something awful," Lucas concurred.

"Are you alright?" Zayna asked.

"No," Lucas admitted. "I had wanted a fresh start. Now, everyone knows what I did."

"Everyone knows what that awful girl did to you," Zayna corrected. "The truth stone showed no lies at Gertrude's story. She doesn't believe you're at fault. You do, and it seems that only you do. People make mistakes. People trust the wrong person. That doesn't make you awful or bad. It makes you human."

"I suppose," Lucas said.

"And I can see you don't believe me. That's alright. You will eventually." Zayna smiled at him.

"How long do you think they'll be?" Gertrude asked.

"Not long," Zayna replied.

"I reckon that they already knew what they wanted to do," Marcus said. "They just wanted confirmation that it was the right choice. Your answers to their questions would have given them that."

"Who rules here?" Lucas asked.

"What do you mean?" Marcus said.

"If your council has that much power, your king or queen must have absolute trust in their abilities," Lucas said.

"King or queen? We do not believe in such tyranny. We choose who rules," Marcus said. "The council is made up of our wisest and best people. Every ten years, we vote on who is the chief. Finn was elected seven years ago. He has led us well in that time. Its seems unwise to let blood and birth decide who makes the decisions for what is best for the people. This leads to unbalance and the potential for disaster for those who have no power."

"Oh," Lucas said. Never had he been happier for having not said he was a prince. He caught Gertrude's eye and she looked intrigued.

"You have no royalty?" she asked.

"No. And I take it you do?" Marcus responded.

"We do," Gertrude said. "As a matter of fact..." she trailed off as she saw Lucas give her a quick shake of his head. "I've met our queen and king, and they are kind and good people." She smiled at Lucas to show she understood.

"Then you have been most lucky," Marcus said. "We have heard tales of war and greed from afar. These are things we've never known here."

"It sounds lovely," she said.

"Almost too good to be true," Lucas added.

Zayna gave him a curious look. She had seen his head shake at Gertrude. She knew he was hiding something. The question for her was what? The door to the council chamber opened and Jerusha stood there smiling.

"Please come back inside," she said. "We have reached our decision."

Tentatively, Gertrude and Lucas entered on Jerusha's heels. They waited until she resumed her seat, and Finn rose to give the council's decree.

"Lucas and Gertrude," he said. "We accept your story and reasons for being here. We give you safe harbour in Coralnoss for as long as you live. Your home can be here with us, and we will give you new purpose." He gestured to Jerusha. "Jerusha is skilled in the magical arts. Lucas, you have our sympathy for your loss. If you wish it, you may resume your learning with our councilwoman."

Lucas looked at Jerusha and saw kindness and wisdom in her face. He nodded. "I thank you," he said. "May I think this over?"

"You may," Jerusha replied.

"Gertrude," Finn continued. "If you wish, you may study our healing arts with Marcus. Perhaps he has methods your mother did not know, and perhaps you have some new ideas for him as well."

Gertrude smiled and dipped into a low curtsey. "We thank you for your generosity and your hospitality. We will take you up on your kind offer."

"Thank you, council, for everything," Lucas added.

"You are most welcome," Finn said, and this time, Lucas saw that the smile did indeed reach his eyes, though the prince suppressed a shiver at the thought that they may have just been welcomed into a gilded cage.

Chapter Eight
Settling In

The days ticked by, and still there was no word from either Gertrude or Lucas. As Navor walked the halls of his parents' home, he was unnerved by how calm Gwendolyn was being. She remained firm in her resolve that wherever her daughter and the prince were, they were together, and they would be alright. She told Navor, when he asked, that they would come home when they were ready.

Navor stopped and rested his forehead against the cool glass of a nearby window. He pretended that it would ease the tension in his skull. He felt as if he were seconds from jumping out of his skin. When they were ready? What did Gwendolyn mean by this? It was as if she was privy to some secret that he hadn't been let in on, and the thought aggravated him as much as it confused him. A nearby noise caught his attention. He turned to see Gerald shuffling down the hall.

"Good day, Gerald," Navor said.

"Ah, hello Navor," Gerald said. "I see you look as pensive as everyone else is pretending not to be."

"You think it's an act for some?" Navor said. He winced at how bitter his words sounded.

"You don't?" Gerald replied. "You know as well as I that people react to stressful situations differently. Some, like your daughter, want to scream from the rooftops over how aggrieved and worried they are. Others, like the Duchess Gwendolyn, bury it deep. They feel as if by pretending they know it will all turn out alright in the end, it will help others around them feel better."

"You think she's pretending?"

"I do," Gerald said. "You show me a mother who says it's alright their child is missing, and I'll show you a liar."

"Gerald, I don't know what I would do without your council."

Gerald chuckled. "I have no intention of letting you find out any time soon."

"I'll hold you to that," Navor said.

Gerald turned to go, and paused, looking back at the king. "I was searching for a cup of tea. Navor, you wouldn't happen to know where I might find one?"

"As a matter of fact, I do," Navor replied. He stepped forward and took Gerald by the arm, leading him down towards the study. They could surely call for a pot once there.

Navor and Gerald entered the study and Gerald let out a contented sigh as he saw the teapot, its spout merrily issuing steam, sitting on a side table with a plate of scones as if they were waiting for him.

"Come, join me in a cup," he said to Navor and he took a seat by the fire.

"I would be most glad to," Navor replied. "Though, I do wonder who this was laid out for,"

"Hmmm," Gerald hummed. "That is a most excellent question. Although, I suppose, if we sit a moment, the recipient will arrive. Until then, I shouldn't think they would mind if we partook."

"I suppose not," Navor said. He took a cup from the tea tray and set about mixing the tea with some milk and sugar, while Gerald kept his black.

The click of the door opening and closing pulled Navor's attention and he looked to see his daughter entering the room.

"Father," she said, seeing Navor sitting by the fire with Gerald. "Hello, Grandfather."

"Audrina," Navor said. "I take it that this tea service was for you?"

"It was," she said. "You know that I skipped lunch. I told my grandmother that I needed to lie down. Swore that I had a headache. But in reality…"

"You wished to be left alone," Navor said. "I understand the sentiment right now. If you wish it, we will leave you."

"No, that's alright," I had my time to myself earlier. I got hungry and so I asked for the tea and scones to be brought here. You're welcome to share, although it seems you already have." She gave her father and Gerald a small smile as she took a seat to join them.

"How are you?" Gerald asked as she poured herself a cup of tea.

"I don't know," she said. "Sometimes it seems as if everything is normal. Other days, it feels as if the world is ending. The worst part is not knowing. I hate it. How can we go on with not knowing where they are, what they're doing, if they're even still…" She stopped and clapped a hand over her mouth. She looked up at her father. "I'm so sorry, Father. I'm trying to remain positive, like Gwendolyn. But it's so hard to do."

"I know," Navor said. "I have to try and believe that we will find them. I do. But sometimes, when it gets quiet, my mind wanders, and it's hard to not be negative. But, your grandfather has sent ships out. They're searching, in case they did go out in a boat."

"They have to have," Audrina said. "I don't know why else we wouldn't have found them yet. The island isn't that big, and we've searched it from top to bottom. But if they did go out on the sea… That night, the storm was so fierce…"

"And your brother is a good sailor," Gerald reminded her in a gentle voice. "And he has his magic."

"You're right," Audrina said. "They could just be lost somewhere, waiting for us to find them."

* * *

Lucas wandered the streets of the island. He found himself fascinated by the people, who seemed equally interested in him. Everywhere he went, people watched him go by. He heard them whispering to one another about the stranger in their midst. He saw what Gertrude had been talking about as he walked through the bustling marketplace. The hair and dress of the people of this island were a kaleidoscope of colour. A few times, he saw a familiar shade of blue, and he felt a twinge of sadness as he thought of the family he had left behind. He shook his head, trying to clear it. He was determined to stick to his plan. Here, it sounded as if he had a true fresh start. Jerusha was offering to teach him, to pick up where his learning had left off. He thought he should take her up on her offer. It sounded as if he might be able to make a new home here. He would not allow himself to get bogged down in melancholy and memories of the home he had left behind.

A small child ran across his path, chased by an older brother. He stopped himself before he tripped over her and couldn't help but smile at her gap-toothed glee as her brother threatened to catch her and tickle her. Unbidden, memories of being chased through castle gardens by Audrina came to mind. His smile turned wistful as he thought of his own sister. He wondered if she was missing him. He knew that she would be missing Gertrude terribly, but maybe that was for the best as well.

"Excuse me."

Lucas turned to see a fruit seller smiling at him. "Hello," he said.

The man looked Lucas over from head to toes and his grin widened. Lucas stared back, taking in the man's shock of bright pink hair. The fruit seller's eyes were the same purple as his own, and he had a wide genial face.

"You're one of the newcomers," the fruit seller stated.

"I am. My name is Lucas."

"Welcome to our island. I'm Mott." He took a bright yellow banana off his cart and handed it to Lucas. "Here," he said to him. "Try one. Mine are the best on the island."

"Oh! Um, I have no way to pay you," Lucas said.

"Nonsense," Mott insisted. "You're new here, and we all want you and your friend to feel welcome in your new home. So, please, as a gift from me to you."

"Thank you," Lucas said. He took the banana, and at Mott's urging, he peeled it and took a bite. "It's delicious!"

"Of course," Mott said. "Tell your friend to come on by. I have one for her too."

"I will," Lucas said. He continued his explorations of the market, meeting merchants and trades everywhere he went. By the time the sun was starting to dip on the horizon, he had been introduced to so many, he knew that all their names would just be a big jumble by morning. But he found himself feeling contented and free for the first time in weeks.

"Lucas!" Zayna called. She had been searching for him for a while now, and seeing him here brought a smile to her face.

Lucas turned and smiled back at her. "Hello, Zayna," he called back.

"What have you been doing?" she asked.

"Gertrude said she was going to be spending the day with your father," he said. "I didn't want to intrude, so I came to the market. I thought that I would do some exploring."

"Oh," she said. Her smile faltered a bit. "I thought that I would show you around."

"I'm sorry," Lucas said. "I didn't realize that I wasn't to go out unaccompanied."

"No, that's not it at all," Zayna said. "You're not our prisoner. I just thought that it would be nice to do this together. That's all."

"Oh," he said again. It seemed that she actually did want to spend time with him. He looked into her eyes. She seemed to mean what she was saying, but a small part of him wouldn't allow himself to trust that. "I'm sorry," he repeated.

"That's okay," she assured him. "Tell me what you did today. Who did you meet? Did you have fun?"

Zayna fell in step with Lucas as he walked back to the council building. He and Gertrude were still staying there. They had been on the island for a few days so far, and everyone seemed to have taken them in. As they walked, Lucas told her about how he had met the merchants, and about how Mott had given him the banana.

"Everyone here seems so open and kind," Lucas said, as they entered the building.

"Aren't they kind where you come from?" Zayna asked.

"Well, I suppose," he said. "I don't think they have a choice when it comes to me." He held his breath as he realized his slip up.

"What do you mean?" Zayna asked. She narrowed her eyes as she looked at him. It was an odd comment to make.

"I…can we talk about something else?" he asked. He hoped she would allow him to change the subject.

Zayna frowned. It was apparent that he was hiding something from her. She knew that his past was a sensitive subject to bring up. Why he felt that people back home had to be nice to him was something she wanted to understand. She just didn't know what had happened to make him feel this way.

"Zayna?" Lucas asked. "I don't want to keep things from you. I just really don't want to discuss this. Not right now anyway. I'm sorry."

"It's alright," Zayna said. "When you're ready, we'll talk."

"Thank you," he said.

"Have you given more thought to the council's offer for you to learn magic with Jerusha?"

"I have," Lucas answered. "I think I want to do it."

Zayna's smile returned to her face. "Lucas! That's wonderful news! It is alright if I send word to them about this?"

Lucas nodded. They entered the council building and Zayna started off down the hall. She paused and turned back to face him. "Why don't you wait for me in the dining hall," she said. "Do you remember where it is?"

"I think so," he said.

"I'll also fetch Father and Gertrude. We can all eat together tonight."

"I'd like that," Lucas said. He smiled at her as he watched her race down the hall, her short skirts fluttering as she moved. He started off in the direction he thought the dining hall was. After their first day there, Lucas and Gertrude had discovered that the council building was built like a giant nautilus shell. The main council chamber was located in the heart of the structure, with the large corridor spiralling out from its door. Here and there, smaller hallways stuck out like small veins, or branches, leading to councillor's offices or smaller meeting rooms. Closer to the entrance to the building, there were some sleeping chambers for workers, or councillors who had been working late. He and Gertrude had been given two of these rooms for them to stay in while on the island. If Lucas remembered correctly, the dining hall was close to the entrance, off a small hallway that struck out to the right.

Lucas wandered down the corridor and was gratified to find that he was correct. He entered the room to find that many of the people who worked in the building had come down for supper. He spotted Finn sitting at a table speaking with a couple of the other councilmen. He met his eyes, nodded a greeting, and sat down at a nearby empty table.

Finn watched Lucas as the boy took a seat. He excused himself from the others at his table and crossed the room. His blue linen robes swirled around him as he walked, and he stopped in front of Lucas.

"May I sit?" he asked the boy.

"You may," Lucas responded.

"I hear you explored our market today," Finn said as he took a seat.

"I did," Lucas said. "How did you hear this? I only just got back." He flushed as he heard himself blurt out his question. He had not meant to sound so accusatory.

Finn smiled. "I have my ways," he said. "It's a small island. People talk, and you are of interest. We don't hear much from the outside world."

"Oh," Lucas said.

"What did you think?" Finn asked.

"Everyone here seems lovely," Lucas said. "You have a beautiful island."

"We do," Finn said." Tell me, Lucas, do you think you could be happy here?"

Lucas eyed the man across from him warily, unsure if this was a trick question or not. He also wasn't sure what an honest answer to it could be. Thinking about it, he remembered how he'd felt watching the sunset. He'd been content. He remembered smiling at the children chasing each other. He remembered Zayna smiling at him. But he also thought about how he felt missing his family, and about everything else that had happened in his life. The pain and sorrow lingered on.

"I don't know," he said after mulling it over for a moment.

"Oh?" Finn asked.

"I don't want to lie to you and just say 'yes,'" Lucas said. "The truth is that I don't know if I can be happy anywhere. Your island here, Coralnoss, it seems as if I have as good a chance as any to be happy here. Probably a better chance here than in most other places. I just have a lot to come to terms with, and I don't know how to do that."

Finn nodded. This boy answered well. He appreciated his honesty on this matter. For him, that showed character, and this was important if he was to find a place for him in their society.

"I hope you don't think me ungrateful," Lucas said.

"Not at all," Finn replied. "Thank you for speaking truthfully. Have you given any thought to our offer of tutelage with Jerusha?"

"I have," Lucas said. "Zayna has actually gone off to tell her that I've accepted."

"Well, this is most welcome news!" Finn said happily. "You will learn a lot from her. I am quite pleased to hear this."

"Thank you once more for your hospitality and your generosity," Lucas said.

At that moment, Marcus entered with Gertrude and Zayna in tow. His eyes widened a fraction as he saw Lucas sitting and chatting with Finn. Finn looked up and waved him over.

"Marcus," Finn said, rising from the table. "Lucas was just telling me the good news, that he wishes to learn magic from Jerusha."

"That is marvellous," Marcus said. "Zayna said the same to me."

"Yes," Zayna said. "Jerusha says that she wishes you to meet her in her study, tomorrow morning after breakfast."

"I will be there," Lucas said with a smile.

"Excellent," Finn said. "Now, I must be off. The council waits for no man."

Gertrude watched him leave, a bemused look on her face. She took a seat across from Lucas.

"I will go fetch us something to eat," Marcus said. "We had a very busy day. I'm sure you're as starving as I am."

"I am," Gertrude said.

"I will help you, Father," Zayna said. She winked at Lucas as she sped off in her father's wake.

"I think she's giving us a chance to catch up," Lucas said with a smile.

"You've been smiling a lot since we got here," Gertrude pointed out.

"Have I?" he asked. "What was your day like?"

"I've learned quite a bit," Gertrude said. "I helped Marcus deliver a baby today. And he taught me a lot about the water plants that grow in the sea, and their various uses. My mother never had access to such things. Her grade was a landlocked one, and it would be interesting to compare the plants here, to what we can find at King Parven's kingdom…"

Lucas gave her a look.

"What?" she asked.

"I don't know how you can do that," he said.

"You mean to stay?" Gertrude said.

"I don't know," he replied. "I have many reasons to. Jerusha will be teaching me magic. I have a fresh start here. I'm making friends. I have no history here. Here, I am just Lucas. People are kind because they *want* to be. Not because I'm a…"

"Prince?" Gertrude finished so him.

"Shh!" Lucas said.

"You haven't told them," she said.

"You heard Marcus," Lucas retorted. "Royals are tyrants. He thinks we're awful. I don't want him to see me that way."

"You don't want him to see you that way? Or is it Zayna who concerns you?" she asked. "You think I haven't noticed how you look at her?"

Lucas rolled his eyes and looked away.

"I understand what appeals to you about this place," she said. "I really do."

"Do you really want to go back?" Lucas challenged. "If you do, you'll still have to deal with Audrina's possible betrothal. What if she does go along with Grandmother's plan and marries some noble idiot?"

Gertrude looked away from him. She didn't trust herself to meet his eyes.

"I thought so," he said.

"Lucas," she said. She hated how her voice wavered. "I don't want to go back and watch the woman I love marry some noble idiot. But at the same time, I can't stay here and let my parents believe I've run off and died, or something equally horrible, or worse. I love them too much to do that."

"I understand," he said.

"Maybe I can write to them and let them know we're alright?" she suggested.

"Maybe…" he said.

"I don't have to tell them where we are even," she continued. "Just that we're alive and well."

"That does seem like the right thing to do," he conceded.

"I will write a letter tonight," she said. "Since you start lessons with Jerusha tomorrow, you can give it to her. She may know a way to get it to Grandfather's kingdom."

"I will," Lucas promised. He was nothing if not reasonable.

Chapter Nine
Lessons

Lucas woke the very next morning feeling nervous and out of sorts. He knew that he had agreed to start learning with Jerusha, but at the same time, learning magic with a new teacher felt like a betrayal to him. He had only ever studied with Kralc, and after his old mentor's death, he had neglected his magic studies. The spells he had used during the storm, in a vain effort to keep himself and Gertrude safe had been the first bits of magic he had tried since the night his home had been burned. He was scared that Jerusha would find him to be a fraud, or that she would not like him.

Lucas hurriedly dressed himself and looked in the mirror. He didn't know why he was so concerned over how he appeared. She wouldn't be teaching him how to dress, and yet he fretted over his reflection, trying to tame his unruly curls into some semblance of order. He growled at himself in the mirror and rolled his eyes.

"This is absurd," he muttered. "She isn't going to care how I look!" With a final glance at himself, Lucas huffed and stepped out into the hallway.

In the hall, Gertrude was also dressed and ready for the day. "Good morning, Lucas," she said. "You're starting your lessons today?"

"Yes, I am," Lucas said.

"Nervous?" she asked him.

"Is it that obvious?" he replied.

Gertrude chuckled. "A little," she admitted. "But only because I know you so well."

"Some days, I hate that you do." He ducked his head and let out a soft laugh.

"I'm sure you'll do fine," she assured him.

"Thanks for your confidence in me," Lucas said.

"Any time you need me, I'm here," she said. "Now, I have something for you." She reached into the pockets of the pants she wore and pulled out a folded piece of paper.

"What's this?" he asked.

"I told you last night that I was going to write a letter to my parents," she said. "I still feel like they need to know we're alright, wherever we are. You said you would ask Jerusha for a way to get it to them."

"I did," he said. He reached out and took the letter from her hand. He held it. It felt heavy. "How long is it? It feels as if you've handed me a whole book's worth of pages."

"I may have spent most of the night writing," she said with a blush to her cheeks. In truth, she had agonized over each word. "I didn't put it in an envelope, or seal it. I have no secrets from you, Lucas. If you would like, you may read it before you agree to send it."

"I couldn't," he protested.

"We both know you will. You can't help yourself. You're very much like Audrina in that way. Your curiosity will always get the best of you." She smiled fondly at the prince and took his arm. "Let's go and find some breakfast."

Lucas grinned at her and let himself get led away.

* * *

Sitting down at the desk, Lucas waited for Jerusha to enter her study. It had taken him several tries, and six different people giving him directions to find the place, but he had managed in the end. He sat with Gertrude's letter sitting in front of him and though he felt weird doing it, he unfolded the papers and set to reading her words.

Dear Mom and Dad— he read.

> *I wish I could tell you where I was. The truth is that I'm unsure as to where that is, exactly. But, I am alive and well. As is Lucas. We set out by boat the night we landed in King Parven's kingdom, and we were shipwrecked by the storm that came upon us. The people on this island are friendly and they have welcomed us both with open arms. I am studying healing with one of the healers on this island, and Lucas has found a new teacher of magic. I feel that it is about time that he resume his studies, and I am glad that this voyage of ours has allowed this to happen.*

I know that what we've done has hurt you both terribly. I know that you probably don't understand why we did it. But, please try. I love you both dearly, and I miss you. Maybe one day I will come home to you. But I cannot in good faith allow Audrina to potentially throw away her kingdom and her people for the love of one person. She has a duty as the future queen of Colonodona. I can't ask her to destroy her future for me. I also cannot stay there and watch her wed another. My heart would break to see it. So, I take the decision out of her hands, by taking myself out of the picture. I am so sorry. I hope that one day she forgives me and understands.

As for Lucas—

Lucas stopped reading and looked up as Jerusha entered the room. He scrambled out of his seat and stood to greet her.

"Good morning," he said.

"Good morning, Lucas," she replied with a warm smile. "I'm glad you agreed to meet with me."

"I am, too," he answered. And he was surprised to find that he meant that.

"What do you have there?" she asked, gesturing to the letter sitting on the table.

"Oh," he said. "My friend Gertrude wrote a letter to her parents. I don't know whether or not it's possible, but it would be nice to find some way to let them know we're alive."

"I understand," she said. She walked over to the table and skimmed the first page. "I think I will look into this. We've never needed to send letters outside of our land before."

"Thank you," Lucas said.

"Good. Now let's start our studies. Tell me what you know about elemental magic…"

* * *

When he finally got back to his room that night thoroughly exhausted, he threw himself down onto his bed and groaned. Jerusha had put him through the wringer. He had been tested on his knowledge of conjuring winds, rain, light, and had shown her his shields. She had complimented him on his work and had given him several large tomes of lore and spells to read over. So far, she had proven to be a patient and knowledgeable teacher, and Lucas had to say he was impressed so far, but he couldn't help comparing her to Kralc.

Where Kralc had been taciturn and grumpy, Jerusha was filled with kind advice and anecdotes about her past experiences. Both Jerusha and Kralc were wise and talented and practised their magic with an ease and fluidity that Lucas envied. However, with Jerusha, Lucas was just another pupil. With, Kralc, there had been a far more personal connection. One that Lucas knew he would never find again. Lucas wasn't certain how he felt about all that had happened. But he knew for certain that he had missed the rush of doing magic well. Each time that Jerusha had complimented him, or told him that he had done a good job, he'd felt a thrill that he hadn't realized he's missed. And that added to his conflicted emotions.

He groaned and forced himself to get up. What he could focus on was the fact that he was not going to sleep in his clothes. It was a minor thing, in context to all he was feeling, but it was something he could sort out right then and there. He peeled off his shirt and pants and folded them and put them aside. He grabbed a nightshirt and pulled it on. Feeling accomplished, he walked back over to his bed and climbed in under the covers. As he lay there, drifting off to sleep, a knock sounded at his door and he grumbled to himself. Why couldn't whoever it was just leave him alone?

"Lucas?" Gertrude's voice sounded from the hallway outside.

Lucas sat up in bed. "What?"

"May I come in?" she asked.

"I guess," he replied.

Gertrude opened the door and came in. She blushed as she saw Lucas sitting there all ready for bed. "I'm sorry," she stammered. "I didn't realize you—"

"It's alright," he said. "What did you want?"

"I know you started working with Jerusha today. I wanted to know how it went," she said.

"You can sit down if you want," he said. He waited until she was perched on the edge of his bed. "I think it went well. It felt good to be learning today. However, it also reminded me of how much I missed Kralc. It was a little weird."

"I understand," she said. "Did you give Jerusha my letter?"

"I did."

"Did you read it?" She looked down and picked at a loose thread in her pants.

"I read the first bit," he admitted.

"Okay," she said. "Thank you for giving it to her. What did she say?"

"She said she would give it to the council. No one has ever really needed to send anything off the island like that," he told her. "She hopes that they can figure it out for you. She understands why your parents and mine need to know we're okay."

"Thank you, Lucas," she said. "I appreciate that."

"Of course," he replied.

"Will I see you at breakfast tomorrow?" Gertrude said.

"I'll be there," he promised. "You're work with Marcus went well today?"

"It did," she said. "Zayna was working with me as well. We make a good team."

"I'm glad," Lucas said. "Goodnight, Gertrude."

"Goodnight, Lucas."

Lucas watched her leave the room and then snuggled deep under his covers once more. Listening to the noise outside in the halls of the building slowly die down as people went home to sleep, he slowly drifted off into a deep, dreamless slumber.

* * *

Jerusha sat in her study. Lucas had long gone back to his room. She sat there and read through Gertrude's letter for the seventh time. She had practically memorized the girl's words by that point. She sat there reading, frowning to herself. One line stuck out like a thorn.

> *Please tell Queen Sitnalta and King Navor that their son is safe. I will take care of him as if he were my own brother.*

That day had gone well between her and Lucas. The boy had taken to her teaching with an enthusiasm she appreciated. But this letter changed things. No. She shook her head. It changed nothing. Lucas had talent and aptitude for magic. She would not let him go so easily. She set the letter down on her desk and called upon her magical energy. Watching the pages burn, she felt a grim satisfaction that she was doing the right thing. This letter was better off having never existed. And if anyone asked her, it never did. She would keep its contents hidden away in the depths of her mind. Finn must never know. Lucas was hers now.

Chapter Ten
Fitting In

Queen Kika found her granddaughter sitting by the water's edge. The princess was dancing her toes over the waves, sitting on the dock in the little cove in the shadow of the castle.

"Audrina," the queen said. She slowly settled down on the dock at her granddaughter's side. It had been some time since she'd done such a thing.

"Good day, Grandmother," Audrina said. She was surprised as Kika settled in beside her.

"I'd forgotten how lovely it is out here," the queen said. She stared out over the sea and let the sea breeze wash over her.

"I suppose," Audrina said. She couldn't see the loveliness. All she saw was the sea separating her from those she loved.

"You're thinking of Lucas," Kika said.

"I am. And also of Gertrude," Audrina felt the sadness deepen. She wished she could tell her grandmother why Gertrude's loss pained her so deeply as well.

"Yes, I understand you and the duke's daughter are close," Kika said. "Such friendships can be hard to come by. Your mother and father are among the lucky few to have people like the duke and duchess in their lives."

"Yes, they are," Audrina said.

"Sometimes, the life of ruler can be a very solitary one," Kika said with a sigh. "We find ourselves surrounded by people, but they are there to serve. I have your grandfather to rely on, and to be my companion, but I can't truly think of someone I think of as a friend. I understand why Gerald stays with you after his loss of Aud."

Audrina found the entire thing rather sad. If Queen Kika lost King Parven, would she become a lonely figure? Her kingdom was far from Colonodona, and she would have no way to see them on a regular basis like Gerald did.

"Grandmother?" Audrina said after a moment.

"Yes?"

"Everyone keeps asking me if I'm alright, and I have to say that I'm really not. Quite frankly, I don't think anyone is right now." She turned to gaze at the queen. Her gently lined face was turned to the sun, and she appeared to be feigning relaxation. "Are you alright? Truly?"

"I—" Queen Kika stopped herself before answering. "Do you know something, Audrina. I don't believe anyone has ever asked me that. At least not someone who was truly interested."

"Well, are you?" Audrina asked.

"No, I'm not," Kika answered. "My grandson is missing. There has been no word from him. We have sailors out and they have found nothing. I fear that he won't be found." She turned to see her granddaughter was crying. "I'm sorry. I know how you feel."

"I don't think they *want* to be found," Audrina sniffed. "Lucas has magic, and Gertrude has her reasons. If they don't want to be found, they won't be."

Kika felt as if she were missing a vital part of the story. "Yes," she said slowly, mulling over her granddaughter's distress. "Your friend did look upset during our dinner. This was the night they vanished. I wonder what could have set her off like that."

"I—" Audrina longed to be able to just open up and speak to her grandmother and to tell her exactly what was going on in her mind and her heart. "I can't," she whispered.

"You can't what?" Kika said.

"I—" Audrina stopped and stared out at the water. Waves lapped at her toes. She tugged at a lock of her long, blue hair that had blown free from her braid.

Kika reached out and pulled her granddaughter close. "You can confide in me," she said.

"Can I?" Audrina asked in a small voice. She swallowed the lump that had formed in her throat.

The queen looked down and met her granddaughter's eyes. "My child, you can talk to me about anything. I'd had hoped you'd know that by now."

Audrina stayed quiet for a long moment. She had been keeping her secret from her grandparents for so long. She had spent all this time agonizing over how they would react. She was so tired of keeping things from them.

"Grandmother," Audrina said. "I know why Gertrude ran away with Lucas."

"You do?"

"Mmhmm." She took a deep breath. "It was because of the conversation you started over dinner. The one where you were asking her mother about finding a nobleman for me to become betrothed to."

"And why would this drive her away?" Kika asked.

"Because…" Audrina took a deep shuddering breath. She couldn't stop now. "Because Gertrude is far more than a friend to me. She loves me, and I love her dearly."

"I don't understand," Kika said. She frowned as she mulled over Audrina's words.

"You were talking to our mothers about my impending marriage," Audrina said. "This is a marriage that I have no intention of going through. I have never wished to marry a man. I love Gertrude." She pulled away and looked at her grandmother. Audrina reached up and wiped tears off her face with her sleeve. "I am in love with Gertrude, and she loves me back."

"Oh," Kika's eyes widened with shock. "But you are the crown princess of Colonodona. How can you choose to do this?"

"But, Grandmother," Audrina said. "This is what you need to understand: I didn't *choose* to be this way. I didn't *choose* to be in love with Gertrude. It is just how I am. Did Lucas choose to be able to do magic? Did my mother choose to have blue hair? Did you choose to fall in love with Grandfather?"

"No," Kika said after a moment. "I also didn't choose to marry your grandfather. I did my duty to my kingdom and to my parents."

"I know," Audrina said. "I understand my royal duty, and I also don't want to be forced into a life of misery. This is more than a loveless marriage. I am not naïve. I understand what wifely duties are, and the thought of forcing myself to do this is something I dread."

Kika sighed. She heard Audrina's words, and she sympathized with her plight. But she also understood what was required of a princess. "And you feel that Gertrude left because she wanted what exactly?"

"She knows that our love will not be accepted by most people. She also knows that, as a princess, I may have to go through a loveless marriage for the good of my people." Audrina pulled away from her grandmother and looked back out at the sea. "Maybe she wanted to take away the choice. Maybe, she felt that if she wasn't here, I wouldn't have to choose."

Kika couldn't help but feel that, if this were the girl's reason for leaving, she was wise for taking the decision out of the princess' hands. A small part of her thanked the girl for putting Audrina and the kingdom above the needs of her own heart. But she also saw her granddaughter's heartbreak, and she understood the pain.

"This whole situation is just so awful," Audrina said. "Lucas feels he betrayed us, and that he lost Kralc as a result of that. He feels responsible. I know that. But as for why he left, I don't know. I know he's been so sad all the time. I know he hasn't been sleeping. He's not thinking clearly. That much was clear to me. I want my brother back." Her words began to pour out of her in a rush. It was as if confiding in her grandmother had opened a floodgate inside her. "I miss the boy I used to tease. I miss my brother so much. The old Lucas. The Lucas who I viewed as a pain and a nuisance, but there was a love there. I hate seeing him hurting. I hate all of this. I hate that that horrid girl Lettie hurt him that way. I hate that his first brush with love broke him and cost him so much. I hate that he felt he had to leave rather than talk to us, talk to me! I hate that he felt he could run away with Gertrude rather than ask for help. I wish I had seen enough to help him. I wish that Gertrude had talked to me about what she was feeling. I feel that they both abandoned me here. I feel lost, and just…and alone. It's not fair. I wish that I could have gone with them." She broke down in sobs, her shoulders heaving, and her breath coming in painful gulps of air.

Kika inched closer to the princess. She reached out and began to rub her back, the way she used to do to her son, Navor. It had always calmed him when he was a child.

"Why does growing up have to hurt so much?" Audrina asked.

"I wish I had the answer to that question," Kika said.

"Thank you for listening to me," Audrina said.

"It sounds like you had that all bottled up for a while," Kika replied.

"I did." Audrina looked into her grandmother's eyes. "How bad do I look?"

Kika took in her granddaughter's blotchy face, and her red rimmed eyes. "I will go in ahead of you. Give you time to compose yourself."

"Thank you," Audrina said. "Grandmother."

Kika paused as she got up. "Yes?"

Audrina chose her words wisely. "I know that you never said you accepted me."

"I—"

"It's alright," Audrina said in a rush. "But thank you for not rejecting me either."

"At the end of the day, you are still my granddaughter, and I am still your grandmother. I love you, and I trust you to do what's right," Kika said.

"But right for who?" Audrina asked.

"That is for you to decide," Kika said.

"Are you going to tell Grandfather what I said?" Audrina asked.

"I will not tell my husband a word of this conversation," Kika answered slowly.

"You think he will reject me," Audrina said,

"I wish I could say he wouldn't," Kika sadly replied. "But he may surprise us. Nevertheless, this is for you to tell him. Not I."

"Thank you again," Audrina said.

"I love you, my child," Kika answered as she walked back up to the castle.

* * *

In the days that followed his first lesson, Lucas found himself thriving. It was as if he'd found a home for himself on Coralnoss. People welcomed him with open arms. They regarded him with a respect he believed he'd earned as the pupil of one of the council members. This wasn't a position he'd been born into. This was one he strove to prove he deserved through his studies and the practise of his magical arts.

On his odd breaks from his learning, he often found himself in Zayna's company. While Jerusha taught him magic, Zayna taught him the ways of the island. She showed him around, introduced him to the people and their culture. He found he was learning as much from her as he was from Jerusha, and he appreciated and looked forward to every second he could spend in her company. The only dark spots in his life on the island were the fact that he missed his family, and that it seemed as if Gertrude were pulling away from him. He made a point of seeing her every day at breakfast, and he spent his evenings with her whenever he could, but she seemed listless and out of sorts. He wanted to help her, to show her that she could find happiness on Coralnoss, as he had, but he felt as if he wasn't getting through to her on that front.

Today, he was given the whole day to himself. Jerusha had bowed out of their lessons, saying that she had important council business to attend to. Lucas had gone to Marcus to ask if Gertrude and Zayna could also be given the day to themselves. He had been happy to, but Gertrude had demurred. She said she wanted to stay useful. She wanted to keep working. Lucas saw right through her excuses. He knew that, by staying busy, she didn't have to think about what was troubling her. He had done that himself, often enough. But he let it slide and had gone off with Zayna.

She had packed them a lunch in a small basket and had led the way to the beach. Spreading a blanket across the sand, the two of them sat side by side looking out over the waves.

"This is where you found me," Lucas said. He lay back on the blanket, basking in the warmth of the sun.

"It is," Zayna said. "I'm very thankful that I did."

"So am I."

"Do you know what troubles Gertrude?" Zayna asked. "You seem so happy here. But she almost appears to be drowning."

Lucas frowned. He had hoped that their day together would be filled with simple pleasures, and shy away from sadness. But it seemed he couldn't escape it.

"It's complicated," he said.

"So uncomplicate it for me," Zayna said. "I like you, Lucas. I like Gertrude, too. I want to be your friend. Both of you. I can see you're both hiding things from me, from everyone, actually. I wish you would just trust me. From what I heard of your story back in the council chamber that first day, I have some inkling as to why you don't. But I want to help you."

Lucas sighed and screwed his eyes shut. He wished he could just trust Zayna. He saw no reason as to why he shouldn't trust her. But he had felt that way about Lettie, too.

And look where that got you. Lucas frowned and told himself to shut up. Zayna was not Lettie. He knew her father. He was here in her land, and he knew exactly where she stood with these people. If anything, he was the stranger here, and she was trusting him, in spite of knowing very little about where he came from.

"Can I trust you?" he asked.

"I certainly think so," she said.

"It's just that what I have to say will colour how others see me," he replied. "Including your father."

"Oh?" Zayna raised a turquoise eyebrow in his direction.

"It will," he insisted. "And I don't want him viewing me the way he views others like me."

"What do you mean 'others like you'?" Zayna asked. She leaned forward, staring into Lucas' warm brown eyes.

"Okay," Lucas said. He took a deep breath. "Gertrude told the truth when she said she left for love."

"I know that," Zayna said. "The truth stone didn't react to her words."

"Yes, but while we didn't lie about anything we said, we also weren't fully truthful. I suppose that a lie by omission may be seen by some as a lie all the same." Lucas sat up and hugged his knees to him. He liked Zayna, and he feared that what he was about to tell her would destroy any chance he had with her.

"I don't understand," she said. She pursed her lips and looked at him. He refused to meet her gaze, staring instead at the waves crashing on the shore a few feet away.

"The one that Gertrude was, is, in love with is my sister Audrina," Lucas said.

"Oh," Zayna said. "Your land doesn't allow such unions?"

"No, not exactly," Lucas said. "I mean, it doesn't recognize them as such. But it's more complicated than that."

"How?"

"Well, here is where I need your word that what I say will go no further." He turned and looked hard at her, his eyes pleading with her to show him he was not making a terrible mistake.

"I swear it to you," she said. "I will tell no one."

"My sister is the crown princess of Colonodona," Lucas said in a hollow voice. "My parents are Queen Sitnalta and King Navor of Colonodona. Gertrude believes that by staying with my sister, she jeopardizes her claim to the crown. She doesn't feel she should make her choose between her and her people, between love and duty."

Zayna gaped at Lucas. "So, if your parents are Queen and King, then you're…"

"The kind of tyrant your father detests," Lucas drily finished for her. "I am a prince."

"That's awful," Zayna said.

"Thanks?" Lucas asked. He wasn't sure if he should be insulted by her comment.

"No!" Zayna gasped, realizing how it had sounded. "I didn't mean that it was horrible that you're a— Oh, I see how you'd think that I…" she groaned and shook her head. "Lucas, what I was trying to say that it's awful how Gertrude and your sister feel that they have to choose between love and duty. No one should ever be placed in such a situation."

Lucas grimaced as he thought back to Kralc. "They wouldn't be the first in my family to be placed in such a situation. And they wouldn't be the first to choose duty."

"I suppose it didn't turn out well for the people you're referring to," Zayna said. She saw the pain in Lucas' expression. "That's what I meant when I said it was awful."

"Yeah," he said. "It is. I wish there was some way I could help them."

"Me, too."

"Gertrude wrote a letter to her parents," Lucas said. "I don't think she wants to leave—" he stopped himself, realizing the fallacy in his words. "No. I'm wrong. She wants to leave. I know she wants to go home, see her parents, see Audrina, and I know that she wants this more than anything. But I don't think she's going to try. She knows her place, or at least what she feels her place is."

"What does she intend to do with this letter?" Zayna leaned forward, fascinated.

"She gave it to me," Lucas said. "I read part of it. Nothing in it gave any hint about where we are. I gave it to Jerusha. If anybody would know how to send word off this island, I figured she would. At least, she would with the help of the council. Was I wrong?"

"You weren't," Zayna assured him. "She would know how to figure out how to send word. But, she won't send it. I promised you could trust me, so I won't lie to you. That letter will never be sent."

Lucas felt betrayed at Zayna's words. "Why not?" he asked. Jerusha had said she would give it to the council. He had told Gertrude that it would be taken care of. She had gone on believing that her parents would have less to fear, knowing they were alive and well.

"I told you our island was a solitary nation," she said. "I know that some of our ways seem odd to you. One of the things you need to understand is that our council has insisted for the past hundred years that we have no contact at all with the other nations beyond our borders. They keep to this ruling with a stringency that seems fanatical to some. But we do not question the ways of the council. It is not done."

"But why?" Lucas asked. "One hundred years of no knowledge of the outside world? That seems absurd. I don't know how you can live with this land being your entire world. Are you not curious at all about what else there is?"

"Oh, I am curious," Zayna said. She grinned at him. "My father says he almost despairs at my continued desire to know what I can about these other lands." She looked at her companion and blushed. "I don't suppose you could tell me some things?"

Lucas almost laughed at the eager look in her eyes. "I can try," he said. A flash of movement caught his eye and he almost jumped in excitement as he saw a woman dive among the waves. He gasped as a long, jewelled and scaled tail flashed behind her. "Mermaids!" he exclaimed.

"Yes," Zayna said with a smile. "Don't you have them where you're from?"

"It has been years since anyone has seen one," he said. "I suppose they wish to stay away. Our ports are so busy with our merchants and their large ships. You would have to go far out to sea to even catch a glimpse of one." He watched, entranced as more and more mermaids surfaced, smiling and splashing about with one another. Their voices carried over to them, a rhythmic, musical series of porpoise-like clicks and squeals. It sounded almost like laughter to him, and he couldn't tear his eyes away from their sparkling torsos, the colour of coral and shell.

"They're beautiful, aren't they?" Zayna asked.

"They are," he said. He felt sad at the thought that his people had chased them away from his shores. His mother used to love telling him stories of mermaids when he'd been younger. She would love to see this.

"You're lost in thought again," Zayna said.

"I'm sorry," Lucas replied.

"Don't apologize," she said. "What were you thinking about?"

"My mother," he answered.

"What is she like?"

"She's wonderful," Lucas said. "She's brave and strong. She's been through so much, and she's lost so many people along the way. But she's still so full of love. She used to make up stories for my sister and me." He smiled at the recollection. "These stories were my everything when I was younger. She would create these worlds for us that were filled with adventure and magic. My sister and I would drive everyone in the castle mad with our antics as we'd act them out. We would go tearing up and down the hallways engaged in battle, or on some treasure hunt or some such thing.

"But sometimes, when she thought no one could see her, when she thought no one was looking, she would get sad. I would see it sometimes, like a veil would pass over her face and she would look as if she wanted to cry."

"Like you," Zayna said. "I'm sorry if I'm overstepping, but you get that way too. Like just now when you were watching the mermaids. You got this look in your eye. You miss her."

"I do," Lucas said. He thought for a moment. Was he that similar to his mother? If so, she was far stronger. She stayed and cared for everyone while he had up and run. "Tell me about your mother."

"I don't remember much about her," Zayna said. "She died when I was quite young. My father says she had the same curiosity as I do. She went out in a boat and came upon a storm. She drowned leaving me in my father's care. He has been my father and mother since then."

"I'm sorry," Lucas said.

"Don't be," she said with a smile. "Marcus has cared for me well. He loves me dearly, and I love him. We've survived."

"I can see that." Lucas let the conversation lapse into silence. He moved over, closer to Zayna and took some grapes out of the basket she had packed. He shifted until their knees were nearly touching. Popping grapes into his mouth, he watched the mermaids as they continued to frolic in the surf.

"They're good, aren't they?" Zayna asked. She smiled fondly at him as she watched him eat.

"They are," he agreed. He settled back into silence and watched Zayna as she ate as well. He found himself comparing her to Lettie. Where Lettie had been all darkness and strength, he found Zayna to be a light, ethereal beauty. She had an energy and happiness the other girl had been lacking. He admitted himself to be entranced by her, and the thought scared him. "It's amazing how similar certain things are here. Although, I have to say that it's odd how little people seem to wear."

"Odd?" Zayna said with a laugh. "You find this 'little'?" She gestured to the dress she wore.

Lucas followed the movement of her hands over her lithe legs. "Y—yes," he stammered. "Back home, men are always wearing vests over their shirts, capes, pants, boots. Women wear gowns that cover every inch of their legs. There are corsets and chemises…"

"Stop," she said. "I understood maybe half of those words. Boots?"

"They're like shoes that go higher up your leg." He stopped as she gave him a blank look. "Shoes? Um, they're like clothes for your feet. You wear them to protect the bottoms of your feet from the roads you walk on. They also can keep them warm and dry."

"But then, you would have less dexterity and balance, would you not?" Zayna asked.

"I don't know," Lucas said. He looked back at the basket of food. "I kind of miss apples," he said as he searched through the food she had packed.

"Apples?" Zayna asked.

"They're fruit that grow on trees. The ones I like are round and red," he explained. "With all the fruits you grow here on the island, I was surprised you didn't have them."

"So, they're like pomegranates?"

"Kind of the reverse," Lucas said. "You eat the skin and the flesh, and leave the seeds of an apple." He allowed the silence to wash over them both once more, while Zayna thought over the ideas of apples and shoes.

"Are you alright?" Zayna asked him, breaking the silence once more.

"I can trust you, can't I?" Lucas asked. He desperately wanted to believe he could.

"Yes," she said. "And I won't tell anyone what we talked about today." She leaned over and placed a chaste kiss on Lucas' cheek. "Let's not be sad anymore," she whispered.

"I'll try," he said. And for once, he meant it.

Chapter Eleven
Gertrude

"Do you have any idea as to how much I love you?"

Gertrude leaned into the warm arms encircling her. She felt safe and content under the shade of the spreading branches of the large oak tree. Birds chirped, and nearby a babbling brook wandered over the stones as it meandered its way around their small farm. Here she was happier than she remembered ever being. Here they could be together, away from the bustling crowd of city life, of castle life, of responsibility and of duty. How she hated those words! And so, they had run away, building a home and a life in their small cottage, on their small plot of land where no one could find them and destroy their peace.

"You never answered my question."

Gertrude smiled and turned to look up into the warm brown eyes she loved so much. She smiled seeing the crown of burrs encircling the princess' head. "I think I do. Audrina, if you love me half as much as I love you—"

"Half?" Audrina playfully slapped Gertrude's shoulder. "Only half?"

"I love you more than I ever thought it possible to love anyone," Gertrude said.

Audrina's eyes lost their sparkle and the day became overcast. The bawling brook stilled, and the warmth of the shade became cold and foreboding.

"If you loved me that much, why did you leave me?" Audrina asked.

Gertrude squirmed, as Audrina's arms closed around her like a vice. "I'm sorry, Audrina…"

"Sorry?" Audrina asked. The crown of burrs shifted and became a crown of gold. Combs grew down, spearing themselves into the princess' scalp. "I'm trapped because of you."

"Audrina, I didn't mean—"

"Didn't mean what?" Audrina cried tears of blood. "Do you think I want this to be my life? I wanted love. I wanted *you*!"

"I'm so sorry," Gertrude cried. "I'm so sorry!"

* * *

Gertrude woke up in a pool of sweat, her face wet with tears. "I'm so sorry," she whispered into the darkness. She lay in bed sobbing softly to herself, grateful that no one could hear. With each day that passed, she realized that she needed to find a way to go home. She wanted the warm advice of her mother, the calm strength of her father, and she wanted to see Audrina again.

Day after day, morning after morning she woke up this way. Each and every night when she closed her eyes, she saw Audrina's face. Every night she heard her voice in her dreams, asking her, begging her for a reason she had left. Every day she regretted her decision more and more.

Gertrude lay in the cooling sheets waiting for the first light of morning to appear through the window of her room. Once it did, she slowly got out of bed and made her way to the small basin of water in the corner of her room. She stripped down and washed herself until she felt sufficiently clean. She dried herself off and dressed for the day. Maybe some work with Marcus would wipe away the sting of her nightmares. Although she knew it rarely ever did.

Making her way into the dining hall, Gertrude saw Lucas wave her over. She sighed to herself. This place had worked wonders on him, and she had to admit that the prince was very nearly the energetic young man she remembered from growing up in the castle alongside of him. She didn't want to take that from him. But it wasn't fair. She felt a wave of bitterness towards him. She wanted to go home. She could see he did not. A part of her wanted to shake him and ask him how he could hurt his parents this way, because she knew that Sitnalta was probably in agony over missing her son. But she knew the pain he'd been in, and she didn't think she could do that. Not yet at least. She had to cling to the idea that her parents knew she was alive, and that she was safe. Until she figured out her next move, she would try to paste a smile on her face and act as if she were happy. For Lucas' sake.

Lucas saw Gertrude approach, and he tried to smile back at her. He saw the dark circles under her eyes, and he could tell her happiness was an act. His smile faltered as she sat across from him.

"Are you alright?" Lucas asked.

"I'm fine," Gertrude said. She tried to stretch her smile wider, as if to show him how alright she truly was.

"Oh," Lucas said. "Did you sleep well?"

"Yes, I did," she lied.

"Gertrude," Lucas said with a sigh. "You're lying to someone who's told these exact same lies too many times to count. I thought we were friends."

Gertrude was hurt. "We are friends, Lucas," she said. She allowed her smile to fall and she buried her head in her hands. "We are friends," she repeated. Her voice was muffled by the sleeves of her shirt.

"Then tell me the truth," he said. "We can see how you're hurting."

"We?" Gertrude asked.

"Zayna sees it, too," Lucas replied.

"You're talking to her about me?" Gertrude said. She looked up sharply at this and felt angry and betrayed. He was talking about her behind her back to someone they barely knew!

"Don't be mad," Lucas protested. "She just mentioned to me that she noticed you seemed sad. You're working with her father, and she wants to make sure you're happy here."

"I understand," she said. "I miss home, Lucas. I miss my parents, and I miss…" she trailed off, not trusting her voice to say Audrina's name.

"My sister," Lucas finished for her. "I know. I miss them, too."

"Do you?" Gertrude snapped. "Because it seems to me that you're doing quite well here without them." She clamped her mouth shut, appalled at how harsh she'd sounded. She hadn't meant to sound like that. "I'm sorry," she whispered.

"Don't," Lucas said. "Don't you dare apologize."

"Excuse me?" Gertrude's eyes widened in surprise.

"I don't care if you think we're no longer friends," Lucas said. He saw Gertrude open her mouth to protest. "You made that clear. You did. But I still think we're friends, and as friends, I care that you're unhappy. And a part of friendship is that we can say what we want to each other, and actually tell each other how we feel, and you just did that. I appreciate it. Don't apologize for your feelings, Gertrude. I did that for far too long, and look where it lead me."

"Here, where you belong," Gertrude said.

"Do you think I belong here?" Lucas said.

"I do. I also wanted to thank you for sending my letter," she said.

Lucas felt a pit form in his stomach. He felt he should tell her what Zayna said about how the letter wouldn't be sent. He had talked to her about the importance of honesty, and he hated keeping something from her, but he also knew it would destroy her if she knew that her parents still had no idea if she were even alive or not.

"You're welcome," Lucas said.

"Are you alright?" Gertrude asked. Lucas had gone a little pale.

"Yes," Lucas said.

"Lucas," Gertrude said. "Seriously? You just spoke to me about telling each other what we feel, how we're thinking. Just as you see through me, I see through you. What is going on?"

"I—" Lucas looked away and saw Zayna enter the room. He smiled, happy for the distraction. "Look! Zayna's here." He waved her over to join them.

"This is not over," Gertrude said. "You will tell me what's going on."

Lucas groaned. There was no escaping this. "I will," he said. "Later."

"I will hold you to that."

"What's going on?" Zayna asked. She looked from one to the other. "Is everything alright with you two?"

"It will be," Gertrude assured her.

"Good," Zayna said.

The rest of the day, Gertrude lost herself in her work. She brewed headache remedies, helped deliver twins, set broken bones, and aided Marcus with all he needed. She was so busy she almost forgot her misery and how dearly she missed the people she loved. More days like this, and she might be able to see how she could fit in like Lucas had. But there was something missing. She couldn't deny it no matter how hard she tried. Home was calling to her, and she knew that she had to find some way to answer.

That evening, over dinner, Lucas was pushing the food around on his plate. He could feel Gertrude watching his every move, and he knew that they would need to talk. He hoped he'd be able to hold off on having this conversation. He just didn't know how to do that.

"Lucas," Gertrude began.

"I know," Lucas groaned.

"Tell me," she said. "I know you're hiding something. You are the worst with secrets. It's obvious to everyone when you have one."

Lucas took a deep breath. He was scared to meet her eyes. "It's your letter," he said.

"What about it?" Gertrude felt a sinking feeling. That letter had been her lifeline.

"I told the truth," he said. "I really did. I gave it to Jerusha. She assured me she would give it to the council, and she said that she would see that it was sent."

"But?" Gertrude said. "There is a 'but' there. You didn't say it, but I know it's there. What is it Lucas? What happened to my letter?"

"Zayna says I was lied to," Lucas said. "She says that this island is so solitary that when they say they have no contact with the outside world, they mean it.

Nothing leaves: no people, no letters, nothing. She says that your letter will never be sent. It wasn't sent. It couldn't have been."

Gertrude wanted to scream. "And you believe her over Jerusha?" she asked in a quiet voice.

"I do," Lucas said. "About this, I do."

"Okay," Gertrude said. She pushed away from the table, and she stood up to leave.

"Where are you going?" Lucas asked.

"I am going to find my letter," she said. "I'm going to ask Jerusha herself about this. Let's see if she can lie to my face." She turned and headed out the door.

"I don't think this is a good idea!" Lucas called after her. But it was too late. She was gone, headed down the hallway to speak to the councilwoman and get some answers.

Chapter Twelve
Secrets and Lies

Ipsinki was feeling torn in two. His only child was missing. It had been a few weeks, and there was no sign of her anywhere. At the same time, the scroll in his hand was demanding his attention and the attention of King Navor and Queen Sitnalta. He needed to speak with them. He came across them both standing over a map, pondering its implications. Navor looked up and waved him over.

"Ipsinki," Navor said. "We were just discussing where our children could be. There's a region to the east of here that is largely unexplored. Our large ships can't sail through there due to the rock walls that render the waters too shallow, as well as the coral reefs. So, we think if we go as close as if safe, we can anchor and send in smaller boats that are easier to steer. There are probably some islands in the region that may be where Lucas and Gertrude can be."

"That does sound like a good plan of action," Ipsinki said. He forgot the scroll in his hand for the moment and regarded the map on the table. "When can we send the ships?"

"As soon as this afternoon," Navor replied.

"Good. However, there is another matter that requires our attention," Ipsinki said. He held up the scroll. "This arrived this morning." He handed the scroll to Navor and waited as he and Sitnalta read its contents.

"I feel awful." Sitnalta frowned. "I knew we were neglecting our duties, but the fact is, we are still the king and queen of Colonodona. There is a massive drought in our kingdom, and we are needed to lead our subjects through it. How can we do that from here?"

"We can't," Navor said dully. "We need to be seen as there for our people."

"That's my feelings on this as well, as much as I hate it." Ipsinki sighed and frowned, torn between the map and the scroll. "My duchy needs me as well."

"The scroll also says that our home is once again habitable," Sitnalta said. "So, we will have a home to come home to."

"I don't see how it can feel like one when our son is missing," Navor argued.

"I agree," Sitnalta replied. "But... Navor, my heart breaks over this. What do we do?"

"If I may," Ipsinki said. "As much as it pains me, we can leave Gwendolyn and Audrina here with King Parven and Queen Kika. They can oversee the continued search for Lucas and Gertrude. We can return to Colonodona and deal with the drought."

Sitnalta rubbed her face. She felt a headache growing in her throbbing temples. As much as she hated this, she knew that Ipsinki was right. She was the queen, and her people needed her. She knew that she had to fulfill her duty to them. But as a mother, leaving here broke her heart. She tried to tell herself that she wasn't giving up on her son. But part of her felt that that was exactly what she was doing.

"We will head home this evening," Sitnalta said in a low voice. "We will leave Gwendolyn, Audrina, and Gerald here to head the continuing search for Gertrude and Lucas. We will find them and bring them home."

"I will attend to the arrangements," Ipsinki said. He left the room, his heart heavy. This wasn't giving up. He had to keep telling himself that though his world had stopped, the rest had kept moving on, and he had to start moving as well.

* * *

Gertrude searched the corridors until she found Jerusha. The councilwoman was sweeping along, her long, silver robes skimming the ground with a grace Gertrude envied. She steeled herself for the confrontation and strode forward.

"Councilwoman!" Gertrude called.

Jerusha stopped and turned. Seeing Gertrude she nodded and waited until the young woman caught up.

"I need to speak with you," Gertrude said. She panted as she stood there facing her.

"What is it?" Jerusha said.

"In private, please?" Gertrude said.

"Alright." Jerusha led Gertrude to her study and gestured for her to enter. Closing the door behind them, Jerusha waited, but Gertrude stayed silent, looking around the room. "What did you wish to speak about?"

Gertrude took a deep breath. It was now or never. "My letter," she said. "I want the truth. Lucas said you would take it to the council and have it sent. But now,

I'm hearing that that would be impossible. I need to know what happened. My parents need to know that I'm alive. I can't bear thinking that they believe I might be dead. It would kill them."

Jerusha saw the pain in Gertrude's eyes. She wished she could help her. "I can't tell you that I sent it," she said. "I apologize, but upon reading your letter, I couldn't hand it over to the rest of the council."

Gertrude's heart pounded. "Why?" she cried. "How could you do that? Lucas trusted you."

"It was for Lucas that I did this," Jerusha said. "Your words put him in grave danger."

"I don't understand," Gertrude said.

"Of course you wouldn't." Jerusha stepped over to a bookcase and pulled out a large, ancient book. "You are strangers to our land and so, you wouldn't know our history. We weren't always as peaceful as we are now. We were once ruled by kings, and they became a tyrannical force, plunging our people into hardship and slavery. They wished to keep us under chain, and our people suffered tremendously.

"Over time, a rebellion rose up against them. They were overthrown and were sent out over the seas into exile. The leaders of the rebellion set up our first council, and we decided that we would never be ruled by a monarchy ever again. Monarchies lead to tyranny and enslavement. This is what we believe. We decided long ago to sever our ties to the outside world, because the world of kings will never understand how we do things. They will see us as a land to be conquered. We cannot, will not allow it." She handed the book to Gertrude and opened it to a page.

Gertrude looked at the painting on the page that Jerusha indicated. Her eyes widened as she saw the king and queen enchained. Their heads were crowned with long, peacock blue hair, their purple eyes were wide with anger. She felt nauseous.

"You understand what I'm saying?" Jerusha asked.

"These people," Gertrude said. "I know people who look like this."

"Your letter called Lucas' parents the king and queen," Jerusha said. "If Finn knew he were a prince, I would lose my pupil, and you would both be—"

"Exiled?" Gertrude asked. She didn't think that would be so bad. In fact, it might mean she could go home.

"Not necessarily," Jerusha said. "Finn might see you as a danger. You could tell the outside world about us. This is something he could never abide." She regarded Gertrude as she stared at the illustration in the book. "The people you know who look like this. Who are they?"

"Lucas' mother has this hair and eye colour," Gertrude said. "She has this man's mouth, his build. I don't know how accurate this picture is, but it's eerie.

Although, I've never seen her with this expression. Sitnalta would never look so cruel. Also, Audrina, she resembles the queen in this picture. But she would also never…" she broke off. Speaking of the princess pained her.

"Audrina," Jerusha said. "This is the one you love."

Gertrude nodded. A tear trickled down her cheek. "I miss her," she mumbled. "I want to go home." She started to cry in earnest. "I'm sorry," she said. "You have all been so kind. But I miss my family, my home, her. I can't…"

"I understand," Jerusha said. "I understand and I am so sorry." She stepped over to her work table and picked up a small clay cup. She filled it with a ruby-coloured liquid and handed it to Gertrude. "Drink," she said.

Gertrude put down the book and picked up the cup. She sniffed it. It had a pleasant fruity smell. "What is it?" she asked.

"It's a cold tea," Jerusha said. "It will help. I promise."

"I don't know," Gertrude said.

"Trust me," Jerusha said. "I only want what's best. Believe that."

Gertrude cautiously took a sip. It had an odd flavour that reminded her of raspberries and something else that she couldn't quite put her finger on. But, in spite of the coldness of the drink, she felt it warm her as it slid down her throat. She drank some more and began to feel dizzy. The cup clattered from her fingers and it shattered across the floor. As she sank down with it, drifting into unconsciousness, she saw Jerusha's face as the councilwoman leaned over her.

"I'm so sorry," Jerusha said. "But you have to know that this is for the best. Lucas is the best pupil I've ever had. I will not lose him because of you. This is nothing personal."

Gertrude cursed Jerusha with her last thought, and let the darkness carry her away.

Chapter Thirteen
Voyage Home

Audrina stood on the docks and hugged her mother tight. "I understand that you have to go," she said with her eyes filled with tears. "I just wish you didn't have to."

"I know, sweetheart," Sitnalta said. She kissed the crown of her daughter's head. "I will write to you every chance I have. I'm leaving you in charge of the search for your brother. I know that you will do everything you can to find Lucas. If anyone can do it, you can."

Audrina nodded. "I promise you, I will," she said.

"Don't," Navor said. He'd been listening in to the conversation. He placed a hand on the princess' shoulder and looked into her eyes. "I know you will do your best, and that's all anyone can ask of you. But please, don't put too much pressure on yourself. That is a promise you can make. Okay?"

"But—" Audrina protested.

"Your father's right," Sitnalta said. "You can't promise for the future. Things happen. All we ask is for you to try your best. You have a good team here backing you up. As much as it pains us all, there are too many unknowns in this situation."

Audrina nodded. "Okay. I promise I'll do my best."

Sitnalta and Navor enveloped their daughter in a tight hug. They kissed her cheeks and walked up the gangplank to their ship.

Gwendolyn watched the king and queen go. She held her husband's hand tightly in hers. She wished that she and Ipsinki didn't have to say goodbye. As much as she loved the princess, her family was Ipsinki and her daughter. She felt them slipping away and she hated it.

"You'll be home before you know it," Ipsinki said. "You and Gertrude. I can feel it."

"I wish I had your positivity," Gwendolyn said. She turned and cupped Ipsinki's face in her hand.

"I'll just have to be positive for the two of us," Ipsinki said. He pulled Gwendolyn in and kissed her deeply. "I love you, and I will miss you terribly."

"And I will miss you," Gwendolyn said. "I love you, Ipsinki."

Ipsinki regretfully pulled away from his wife and walked towards the ship. Once on board, he watched as Gwendolyn moved to stand at Audrina's side on the dock. The soldiers lifted anchor and with the king and queen at his side, he stood and watched as his wife grew smaller and smaller as they sailed away. He stared until she had disappeared from sight, and still he couldn't bring himself to leave that spot on deck. He clung to the hope that the next time he saw her, his daughter would be reunited with them as well.

He didn't know how long he stood staring out at the waves as the island vanished, but a soft hand pulled him away from his staring and he looked to see that Sitnalta had joined him. She had plunged into planning and had been trying to stay busy while on board, keeping her mind off of everything.

"We need to discuss our plan of action when we arrive," she said. "Navor wants to know what the food stores are stocked with in your duchy."

"Of course, my queen," he said.

She laughed. "It still sounds strange to hear you call me that," she said. "I don't know how I can still laugh. It feels so wrong to be capable of it."

"I know what you mean." Ipsinki frowned. "Gertrude hated our voyage to see you. Every second of it she was plagued with seasickness. I don't understand how she would have gotten onto a boat with Lucas. It boggles my mind. I keep going over it and over it in my mind." He rested his arms on the rail of the ship and stared out at the slowly darkening sky.

"She would have done it to stop my son," Sitnalta said. "I feel like such a bad mother. I saw how he was hurting, and I deluded myself into believing that all he needed was time. Time to work through it all. I did, after all. After I lost Aud, after all that had happened with Sparrow, I worked through it. I'm still working through it. I knew he probably blamed himself. I just thought that he would talk to me in time, and so I gave him space. I am so sorry, Ipsinki."

"Don't," Ipsinki said sharply. "Don't you dare blame yourself for any of this. I don't. You love your children just as I love my daughter. They both know it. Lucas knows it. Audrina knows it. You are not a bad mother."

"I feel like one right now," Sitnalta said. "I feel as if I'm choosing between being a bad mother or a bad queen. I feel I'm choosing wrongly right now."

"I know exactly how you feel," Ipsinki said. "I feel as if I'm doing my duty to my people, but my heart is on that dock with Gwendolyn. I trust her to do what's right and to find our children, but I feel like a terrible husband leaving her to do it alone. I just…" he trailed off, raising his hands to flail helplessly in the air.

"She's not alone," Sitnalta said in a whisper. "I left her Audrina and Gerald." She sighed. "I just wish that I had done more before he felt it had to come to this."

"You couldn't read his mind," Ipsinki said.

"No. I couldn't. But don't you feel that parents should?" She smiled a mirthless smile. "It would make being a parent so much easier."

"Or harder," Ipsinki dryly replied. "I don't need to know every moment my daughter thinks that she hates me, or that I'm being unfair."

"Hmmm. I suppose Audrina thinks that about a dozen times a day about Navor and I," Sitnalta conceded. "It's probably best I don't know about it."

"Probably." Ipsinki looked down at the water. "If Gertrude had gone to stop Lucas, or to find some way to help him, I would have thought that she would have found some way to contact us by now."

"She will," Sitnalta said. "If that's why she went, I believe she will."

* * *

Lucas approached his lesson with a growing feeling of trepidation. Gertrude had run off from breakfast hell-bent on confronting Jerusha about her letter, and Lucas didn't know what he expected to come from that. He knew that he was not to blame for this, but at the same time, he didn't know Jerusha well enough to know what to anticipate as the fallout. When Kralc had been irritated, it usually meant a lesson filled with being made to re-alphabetize the potion ingredients, or resort the scrolls by subject. On one occasion, Lucas had been sent home rather than be taught at all. What he'd seen of Jerusha's manner, Lucas didn't think this was her way. But still, he approached the door to her study a jangle of nerves.

"Jerusha?" Lucas called. He entered the room to find it empty, and his heart sank. Until now, she had always maintained an air of punctuality. As he walked towards the large worktable in the centre of the room, he cried out as he stepped on something, and a sharp pain lanced through his foot. "Damn!" he hissed and hopped up to take a seat on a chair. "This is why we wear shoes back home!" He examined the sole of his foot, and his eyes watered as he saw the shard of pottery embedded in the skin. Gritting his teeth, he slowly and carefully pulled it out. He needed to find some way to staunch the blood that now flowed freely. He looked around helplessly. He hadn't thought this through. If Gertrude was there, she'd know what to do. But he was alone.

The soft padding of footsteps approaching caused Lucas to pause. He let out a grateful whimper as he saw Jerusha enter the room.

"What happened?" Jerusha cried as she took in the sight of her pupil perched on a chair, blood dripping from his foot.

"I don't know," Lucas said. "I stepped on something. What broke in here?"

Jerusha rushed over and grabbed a rag. She tied it tightly around his foot in an attempt to get it to stop bleeding. "Stay here," she said, her voice low and tight.

Lucas watched her rush out of the room. In moments, she was back at his side.

"I have sent someone to fetch Marcus," she said. "He will examine your wound. I think you can have the morning off."

"I—" he paused. She seemed upset, and he had a strange feeling that it wasn't just his injury that was causing it. "Jerusha, did Gertrude come and see you today?"

Jerusha frowned. Her lips were pressed together in a thin, pale line. She took a breath before answering. "She did."

"I spoke to her this morning," he said. "She ran off pretty upset."

"Lucas, did you tell her that I wouldn't have sent the letter?" Jerusha asked.

"I'd heard that this was a possibility," Lucas said. "I don't like lying to people I care about. I've learned that only leans to trouble."

"An admirable sentiment," Jerusha said with a sigh. "She was here, quite agitated. I gave her a drink, and when I told her that I didn't send the letter, she grew quite irate and smashed my cup. I'm sorry, I thought I'd cleaned up all the pieces." She gestured to his foot. "It seems I was wrong. "She stormed off, and I'd gone after her when you arrived."

"I see." Lucas closed his eyes and breathed deeply. His foot was throbbing terribly. "Jerusha, why didn't you send the letter?"

"Ah yes, I knew you would ask that. I didn't send it to protect you," she said with a fond smile. "I feared that if Finn read what was in there, he would take you from me." She rose and plucked a book off the table. "This is what you can do today. Read this book. It contains our history, and I believe, your connection to it. Finn can never learn who and what you are."

Lucas reached for the book but paused as he saw the blood staining his hands. "Maybe I should wash first," he said, grimacing in distaste.

"That would be wise," Jerusha agreed. She rose and fetched a basin of water and some rags and stood at Lucas' side as he cleaned his hands.

Lucas took a dry cloth and began to dry himself off as Marcus came into the room. He carried a satchel with him and instantly knelt in front of Lucas.

"What did you do to yourself?" he asked.

Lucas shrugged. "I stepped on this broken shard of crockery," he said, indicating the bloody piece on the table.

Marcus carefully unwrapped Lucas' foot and carefully examined the wound. He nodded to himself and opened his satchel. "I'm going to need to stitch this up," he said.

"Do what you must." Lucas gripped the edge of the table hard in anticipation of the pain.

Marcus took a small vial and poured it over the wound. He heard Lucas hiss loudly and murmured words of apology. Taking a curved needle and a spool of silk thread, he started to work. With steady hands, he sewed the wound up quickly, and neatly bandaged it once more.

Lucas was pale faced and shaking, but whatever Marcus had done had lessened the pain to a dull burn. "Thank you," he said in a weak voice.

"Stay off of it for a day or so," Marcus said. "Can you spare him, Jerusha?"

"Whatever he needs," Jerusha replied. "I can have someone help him to his room. He will be better at resting there."

"Good." He turned back to Lucas. "Have you seen Gertrude? She never arrived at my hut this morning, and I was expecting her."

Lucas shook his head. "Not since breakfast."

"She came to see me," Jerusha said. "I'm afraid we had a disagreement. She left here rather upset. I'm sure she will turn up eventually."

Marcus nodded. "Thank you, councilwoman. Stay off your foot, Lucas. It will heal faster that way."

"I will." Lucas watched him go. "Can I stay here and read a while, Jerusha? I'm a little shaky at the moment. I can have someone help me to my room later."

"Of course," Jerusha said with a smile. She turned and fetched a cup and a pitcher of water. "Have something to drink. It will help you."

Lucas took the offered beverage and drank down the cool water gratefully. "Thank you."

Jerusha nodded and slid the book over to him. "I will leave you in peace. I have some council business to attend to."

Lucas watched her go and opened the book to the first page. No one was angry with him, Gertrude would turn up soon. Everything would work out just fine. He had nothing to fear, and no worries to plague him.

Chapter Fourteen
Responsibilities

Sitnalta swore she could still smell the smoke leeching from the stone walls of the castle. It seemed to burn her lungs and sting her eyes as she walked to her newly rebuilt sitting room. The masons and carpenters all assured her that her home was habitable, though work was still being done on several rooms. She and Navor had been welcomed back with open arms by their servants the instant they had ridden through the castle gates, and though she felt a pang that they had done so without their children, she had to admit that it felt good to be back.

Walking through the corridors of the castle she had been taken aback at how bare everything looked without their old tapestries and the vases of flowers. She quickly instructed people to gather bouquets and to place them around the castle. She needed colour. She hoped that it would be enough to lift the mood in the place. When everything was sorted, and when both Audrina and Lucas were home, then they could go about restoring art to the walls, and their home to a sense of its former splendour.

She steeled her shoulders and entered her sitting room. A brand-new mahogany desk stood proudly to one side. Two embroidered armchairs sat in front of a newly carved stone hearth. She nodded upon seeing that the hearth was cold. No fire burned within. For that, she was grateful. A chill crept up her spine as she remembered how the flames had burned the last night she had been there. She walked over to her desk and saw that maps and lists had already been laid out for her. Her servants had done well at acquiring all she needed.

"Sitnalta," Navor called.

"I'm already in here," she answered.

Her husband entered the room to find his wife taking notes on a piece of parchment. "Right to work?" he asked.

"Of course," she said. "It looks as though our stores are nicely full. We should have ample food if we ration. This, and our neighbours should honour our treaties with them. If we're careful, we should be able to weather this drought. We need to be kind to the farmers who will be short during this time."

"Tax cuts should ease their burden. We all need to make sacrifices so we all pull through," Navor said.

"I agree," Sitnalta replied. "I will draft the necessary decrees. We will stay through all of this, and Ipsinki is already on his way to his home. Our people need to see us doing our best for them all. Once these are written up, we will have them sent to all the dukes and to our neighbours."

"And then?" Navor asked.

"And then, I shall write to our daughter. Tell her we've arrived safely." She yawned widely. "Afterwards, I shall get some much-needed rest."

"I think I will join you." Navor pulled one of the chairs to the other side of the desk. "I will write half of these decrees. Half the work means half the time."

"Whatever would I do without you?" Sitnalta asked with a smile.

"You never need to find out," he assured her.

* * *

Lucas read through the book Jerusha had left him with a growing sense of dread. He could clearly see his family in the illustrations of the cruel monarchs who had enslaved the people of Coralnoss. Their eyes, the same vivid purple of his own, their hair, the same peacock blue that had delineated the royalty of his mother's line; these things leapt out at him from the pages. They had been exiled for their crimes, only to establish a new royal line in Colonodona. But it seemed as if their cruelty had petered out over the generations. His mother was no tyrant, and his grandmother, Learsi had been known for her love and compassion. Yet he doubted that Finn would see reason if he knew that a descendant of these monsters was living among them and had the ability to perform magic.

The light in his room was growing dimmer. Whispering a spell, Lucas set the candles in his room ablaze. He smiled to himself. Under Jerusha's tutelage he was growing stronger. Conjuring fire, wind, levitation of objects, all was becoming second nature to him. He liked to think that Kralc would be proud of all he had accomplished in his time on Coralnoss. He liked it there, and had begun to think of it as his new home. He just wished he could find a way to make Gertrude see it as such as well. Perhaps there was a spell? He frowned, not liking where his mind was going. He would not use magic in such a way. It would be a horrible violation to control her thoughts and emotions like that.

A knock sounded at the door and Lucas smiled. There she was. They would talk this out, and she would see reason eventually. He could always have her write a new letter, one that did not allude to his royal status back home. Then, surely Jerusha could send it for her. That would fix everything.

"Come in," Lucas called.

The door opened to reveal not Gertrude, but Zayna holding a tray of food. "I thought you might be hungry," she said as she came in, closing the door behind her.

"I am," Lucas said, his stomach rumbling. He'd been so engrossed in his book, he'd forgotten all about the needs of his body.

Zayna carefully set the tray on Lucas' lap and sat on the edge of his bed. "How are you feeling?" she asked. "My father told me what had happened to your foot. I suppose that this is one of the reasons your people wear those shoe things you told me about."

Lucas laughed. "It is. If I'd been wearing them, it would have spared me most of the damage and pain."

Zayna winced in sympathy. "Is there anything else I can do for you?" she asked.

Lucas shook his head. "I wouldn't mind the company," he said. "Did Gertrude ever meet up with your father? I know she was supposed to be working with him today. I'm a little bit worried. She had a falling out with Jerusha over her letter. I…I told her that you said the council would never send it."

"Oh dear," Zayna replied. "No wonder she ran off. No. She never arrived. But, give her time. Maybe she needs to sort this out on her own. She'll turn up. It's a small island. Where could she have gotten to? She'll be found when she's ready."

"I suppose." Lucas frowned and looked at the food. He picked up a small braided loaf of bread and started ripping into it. He ate in silence a few minutes thinking everything over.

"You're lost in thought today," Zayna said.

"I have a lot to think about," Lucas replied.

"Such as?"

"I found out that my ancestors were the monarchs that enslaved your people," Lucas said. "I'm not sure what to make of that. Is it really a coincidence that the storm brought me here? I ask myself that, and then I realize that this sounds crazy. But at the same time…"

"Whoa," Zayna said. "How is that possible?"

Lucas picked up Jerusha's book and handed it to Zayna. He showed her the painting in it of the king and queen being sent into exile. "This looks just like my mother and grandmother. My family is the only one in our land with hair like this and eyes like this. You heard what Gertrude said about the people from Colonodona. And here, on this island…"

"She talked about our colouring. I remember," Zayna slowly replied. She stared at the painting and then looked into Lucas' eyes. "Your eyes are just like the queen's, and the shape of your mouth…" she reached up and lightly traced Lucas' lips with her fingertips.

Lucas shivered at her touch, his hunger for food forgotten. "No wonder Jerusha didn't want Finn to read Gertrude's letter," he whispered. "What would he have done to me if he knew?"

"Let's not think about that," Zayna said. "You're safe here and now. I will help keep you that way."

"Zayna," Lucas breathed. "I should very much like to kiss you."

"And I should very much like you to," she said, and leaned forward, closing the distance between them and catching his lips with her own.

Lucas reached up and tangled his fingers in her long, turquoise hair. He kissed her, revelling in her warmth and softness. When they broke apart, he saw she was smiling at him, and her eyes sparkled in the candlelight.

"Thank you," he said and blushed, feeling foolish.

Zayna laughed. "I am quite fond of you, Lucas," she said. "I have no intention of letting you go. Finn will have to get through me to get to you."

"I won't let it come to that," he said. "The only people who know who I am are you, Jerusha, and Gertrude. Let us keep it at that."

Zayna nodded. "Gertrude will come around. We will make her see that this island can be a place of belonging."

"I think that if it's a letter she wants, she can send one," Lucas said. "Just don't mention kings, queens, or princes in it."

"We just need to find her and explain," Zayna said. "If she doesn't come home tonight, I will search for her tomorrow morning."

"Thank you." Lucas cupped Zayna's cheek in his hand. "For everything."

Zayna leaned forward and kissed him again. "And thank you, Lucas," she told him. "Thank you for finding our island."

Chapter Fifteen
The Missing and the Left Behind

Audrina sat on the bench on the dock, her mother's letter clutched in her hand. She was glad that things were going well at home. So far, her mother and father's rationing plans were working out to everyone's favour. The farmers were all well-protected from financial hardships, and Colonodona's allies were sending aid through this hard time. Sitnalta had asked for news as to how the search for Lucas and Gertrude was coming along. It bothered her deeply that she had no new reports to send to her mother. She wished she could write to her and tell her that they had leads. She wished that she could send word that they had both been found, but there was no news. No trace of them had been seen anywhere. Audrina felt as if she were living on tenterhooks. She wanted her life back, but everything was put on pause, and she didn't see how she and her family could continue on with their lives as if things were normal, when it was plain to see it was impossible. Nothing was normal. She didn't know if it ever would be again.

Back at the castle, she knew that her grandparents were preparing for some guests. She understood that people who ruled needed to continue to act as if it were business as usual, but she did not know how they could entertain anyone right now. She had been asked to join them when she was ready, but she didn't want to fake a smile, and put on good cheer.

"Audrina," Gwendolyn called as she came down to join the princess. "King Parven and Queen Kika are asking about you. They wish for you to join them."

Audrina sighed. "I know," she said.

Gwendolyn took a seat beside the princess. "I should warn you before you go in there," she said.

"Oh?"

"Yes." Gwendolyn looked at Audrina with a sad smile. "There is a lovely young man with the duke and duchess that are visiting. Their son, Salazar. Your grandfather was giddy with delight upon meeting him."

Audrina groaned. This was worse than she'd first thought. "And what of my grandmother?" she asked. "How 'giddy' was she?"

"The queen was…" Gwendolyn struggled to find the right word for it. Queen Kika's behaviour had not been what she'd expected from her. "Let's call it 'coolly formal.' She was quite polite, but very reserved." She regarded the princess carefully and saw the corners of Audrina's mouth curl upwards a fraction in the semblance of a smile. "You told her about you, didn't you?"

"I did," Audrina said. "I didn't think she'd understand. I'm still not sure she does, but this is hopeful."

"It is." Gwendolyn rose from her place and held her hand out to the princess. "Shall we face the gauntlet together?"

"We shall," Audrina said and walked up to the castle on Gwendolyn's arm.

In the castle, Audrina allowed herself to be escorted into the salon by Gwendolyn. She saw her grandfather in deep conversation with a man who appeared to be around the same age of her father. This man was smiling and had dark, laughing eyes. He seemed kind enough, but her attention was drawn to a young man with long black hair and a sullen expression. She turned to Gwendolyn and shook her head.

"I suppose that boy is the famous Salazar?" she said, her voice deadpan.

Gwendolyn couldn't help but snicker. "He doesn't stand a chance against you," she said.

"Oh, Gwendolyn," she said. "I'll go easy on him. None of this is his fault." Audrina held her head high and walked over to where her grandmother was speaking to Salazar's mother. "I hear you were asking for me, Grandmother," she said, keeping her voice light and her expression sweet.

"Yes, Audrina," Kika said with a relieved look on her face. She had been worried about Audrina's reaction to their guests, but it seemed as if the princess was minding her manners. At least for the time being. "I would like to introduce you to the Duchess Marya. Duchess, this is my granddaughter, Princess Audrina."

Audrina inclined her head in Marya's direction. "Welcome. It is a pleasure to make your acquaintance. It is always lovely to meet people from my grandparents' kingdom."

"The pleasure is mine, Princess," Marya said. "I was most saddened to hear about your brother's disappearance. If there is anything we can do…"

"Thank you for your offer," Audrina said with a sad smile. "I may just take you up on it, if you don't mind. I do have some ideas as to where he and the Duchess Gwendolyn's daughter may be. There is an area to the east of here that our ships cannot go."

King Parven heard Audrina speaking with Marya and excused himself from his conversation to go and join the women. "Audrina," he said. "Let me handle this matter. Why don't you go and introduce yourself to Marya's son, Salazar? I'm sure you young people would love to get acquainted and leave us to our boring conversations."

"I'm sure I wouldn't, Grandfather," Audrina replied, her tone dripping sweetness. "We were discussing my brother Lucas, and there is nothing that bores me about this. In fact, this is why my parents left me here. I would not want to let them down. A princess must do her duty, and this is the one they left in my hands."

King Parven shot his wife an anxious look, and Kika feigned ignorance of it. She reached out and subtly gave her granddaughter's hand a squeeze in support.

"This is an admirable trait in a woman," the duke said coming to join them.

Audrina found herself squirming under his scrutiny. "Hello," she said, looking up at him. "I trust you had a pleasant journey."

"I did," he replied with a genial smile. "You must be King Parven's granddaughter. He has been singing your praises for some time. I see he has not exaggerated one bit. I am Duke Marius." He turned to the boy lingering in the corner of the room. "Salazar! Come and meet the princess."

Salazar slowly sidled up to them, and timidly extended his hand to Audrina. "Hello, Princess," he whispered.

"Hello, Salazar." Audrina struggled to keep from giggling. This was her grandfather's idea of an eligible young man for her?

"Why don't you go and get acquainted?" Mary asked her son with a gentle smile.

Salazar sighed and looked up into Audrina's eyes. He looked nervous. She gave him and encouraging smile and held out her hand. "Shall we walk? I can show you my favourite place to sit."

Salazar gave a tiny nod of his head and allowed her to lead him out of the room. She was mildly surprised to find him a head shorter than she was, and he seemed as if he were liable to jump out of his skin at any moment. As soon as they were out of earshot of the room, and outside the castle walls, he stopped walking and turned to her. "Please don't take this the wrong way," he said. "I really don't want to offend you, but I have no intention of marrying you."

Audrina couldn't help herself. She burst out laughing at his statement. "Oh!" she exclaimed. "Salazar, here I was afraid of offending *you*!" she chortled.

Salazar was gobsmacked. "I'm sorry?" he asked.

"Salazar, come with me, and let's talk."

Salazar walked with the princess down to what she had come to think of as "her" bench on the dock. She sat close to him so she could hear his quiet words over the sound of the waves. She waited until he seemed as comfortable as he was going to get and then she cleared her throat.

"Here I was, prepared to tell you that I had no intention of marrying you," she said. "And you had to go and beat me to it."

Salazar felt a great weight lift off of his shoulders. "Thank you. I just—thank you."

"So, do you have someone stashed away in your duchy?" Audrina asked. She knew she was being nosy, but she felt giddy with relief. A co-conspirator, someone on her side, this was someone she could work with. Anything to keep her grandfather off her back.

"What? No!" Salazar frowned. How could she possibly understand his dilemma?

"It's alright," Audrina said softly. "You think you're too young for marriage?" She watched him squirm. "I think we can help each other. If you let me. I'll tell you my secret if you tell me yours. Okay?"

Salazar looked at Audrina. He'd been led to believe he was wrong somehow. At least, that's how his parents viewed him. Here was someone who seemed to want to know, to *understand*. He just didn't think it was possible.

"Maybe I just don't want to marry you," he mumbled.

"And maybe I don't want to marry anyone," Audrina countered. "Not now, not ever."

Salazar looked up at the vehemence of her words. Maybe she did understand. "Maybe, neither do I," he conceded.

Audrina let out a breath. "Okay." She looked out at the water. "My brother is missing. And Gertrude is with him. She's the Duchess Gwendolyn's daughter. Gwendolyn is the woman who came into the room with me." Seeing his nod, she continued. "What I'm about to say can go no further. Gertrude is why I won't marry. Not for politics or any sense of duty. It would be wrong. I won't have a loveless marriage. Not when I know what love is. I love Gertrude."

Salazar's heart sank. She didn't understand.

"What's wrong?" Audrina's saw the shift in Salazar's expression.

"Maybe my parents are right," he said. "Maybe I am wrong."

"About what?"

"I won't marry because I know what marriage entails, and the whole thing seems wrong to me. I have no desire for it, for anyone. I know what I would have to do with a wife, make heirs, and the whole thing just isn't me. I've never had an interest or desire for women. I've never understood it. It's just…" he trailed off looking helplessly at Audrina, hoping she'd understand.

"We have our captain back home, a man named Micah." Audrina smiled fondly thinking of him. "He has been with the same man for years. They are deeply in love."

"No," Salazar said. "Not for me."

Audrina pondered this for a moment then smiled. "That's fair. I've come to believe that people are people. The world is a big, beautiful, scary place. And in it, there are all sorts of people with all sorts of desires and needs. This doesn't make them wrong. It makes them human, Salazar. So, tell me, what do you want from people?"

Salazar gave Audrina the first genuine smile she'd seen from him and it lit up his face. His eyes, she saw, were blue like the sea, and they shone at her. "I want friendship, understanding, and companionship."

"This I will gladly give you," she said.

"I want someone who will support my interests. I like to study the sea and I love boating and I read the histories of the sailors. Many of them kept diaries. What do you want?" he asked her.

"From you? I would like the same." She turned back to the sea. "Otherwise, I want my brother back, and I want Gertrude. I think you might be able to help me."

* * *

Lucas was up and about once more. True to Marcus' word, his foot healed nicely and though he was walking with a slight limp, he was happy to once more be able to walk to Jerusha's study, and to join Zayna and Marcus in the dining hall for meals. The one dark spot was that Gertrude had still not returned. He felt a slow grinding worry settle in. Something was not right, he just didn't know what that was.

He made his way through the corridors after a short break in the day. Jerusha had gone off to meet with Finn and had given him some time to go and feed himself and take a short break in their work. Now he was winding his way back, and his face split wide into a smile as he saw Zayna wave at him. He stopped and she ran over.

"How has your day been?" she asked. Her hand reached out and her fingers twined with his.

His face flushed at the contact with her. "My day has gone well," he said. "Jerusha and I are working on elemental magic. Manifesting rain, helping crops grow, that sort of thing."

"That's fantastic," Zayna said with a smile. "My father says that Jerusha has wanted help with this for some time. It's been a lot for her being the only one on the island helping us through her magic."

Lucas nodded. "Back at home, the wizards aren't really used for such things. At least, not in Colonodona. Our kingdoms are far too large for one man, or woman to be in charge of such things."

"So what do they do?" Zayna walked with Lucas, keeping pace with him as he slowly limped along to Jerusha's study.

"Well." Lucas scratched his head. "Honestly, the only one I knew was my old mentor, Kralc. He liked to keep to himself, and to stay out of other people's business." He paused. The pain that he usually experienced when he thought about the wizard, or spoke about him felt like a dull ache, instead of the kind that would knock the air from his lungs. Maybe it was due to the fact that he was actually opening up to people. Maybe it was because he was honouring him by continuing his studies. Lucas was not sure. "Kralc was someone who valued his privacy and liked to stay on his own. He didn't trust people as a rule."

"Why not?"

"He'd been hurt in the past." Lucas paused and looked at where they'd wound up. He opened the door to Jerusha's study and peered inside. She hadn't returned from her meeting yet. "Come inside with me?"

Zayna nodded and followed Lucas into the room. He closed the door behind them and took a seat at the table to take the weight off of his foot for a bit.

"Why do you think he didn't trust people?" she asked, leaning on her elbows on the tabletop.

"He lost the one person he loved." Lucas stopped as he said those words, finally realizing the fallacy of the statement. Now that he'd said it out loud, he saw that it just wasn't true.

"What is it, Lucas?"

"No. He didn't. He thought he had, but he didn't." The pain he'd thought had healed came rushing back. His eyes filled with tears as he saw the truth. "Kralc fell in love with my mother's mother. She was the love of his life, and as a princess, he let her go so she could save her parents and her kingdom. But that wasn't right. He left her with something." He thought of the stubborn set of Kralc's jaw, and of the shape of his mouth when he had smirked at him, or the few times he saw him genuinely smile. He saw those same lines, and those same traits every time he looked in the mirror. "He left her with my mother. Lettie told me as much when she was getting me to do her bidding. That was why he came out of seclusion to teach me… I…" The tears fell fresh. "He loved me. He died to save us because he loved us."

"Oh, Lucas." Zayna put her arms around Lucas and let him cry. He cried until he was spent.

"I knew, and I never told him I knew. And now it's too late."

"I know about too late." Zayna took a handkerchief and handed it to Lucas. "My father is filled with 'too lates' from my mother. It seems that whenever we lose someone, every day has several too lates in it. Doesn't it?"

"Yeah, it does." Lucas leaned into Zayna's embrace. "I need to find Gertrude. I have to send her home. Our grandfather, Kralc, he lived his life with a slew of too lates and I won't let my sister's life wind up the same way. She and Gertrude deserve better. As much as this island has been a sanctuary for me, it is not what she needs."

Zayna nodded and kissed the top of Lucas' head. "I agree," she said. "I'll go and keep asking around. Someone somewhere must have seen her, and we can figure this out together. We can find a way to get her home."

"Thank you," Lucas said, and he pulled her in for a kiss. He broke away from her as the door to the room opened.

"Hello, Lucas, Zayna," Jerusha said as she entered. "I see I'm interrupting." She gave them a knowing smile as she swept into the room.

"Uh…" Lucas managed to squeak out.

Zayna laughed. "I'm sorry, councilwoman. I was just leaving. Lucas, I will speak with you later."

"Yes. Um, later." Lucas knew he was blushing terribly. His face felt hot under Jerusha's stare. He watched as Zayna left.

Jerusha looked Lucas over. His eyes were red-rimmed, and it was clear that he had been upset. Her smile faltered as she saw the state of him. "Are you alright, Lucas?"

"Hmm?" Lucas looked up at the question. "Yes. I'm alright. We were just talking."

"About something sad, I see."

"We were just talking about my old teacher." Lucas looked into Jerusha's eyes and saw compassion there. "It's just that I miss him, and I always will. What most people don't know is that he was more than my teacher. He was my grandfather as well. But that was a secret. No one in the kingdom knew."

"I see." Jerusha looked at Lucas as if she were processing some new revelation. "So, magical abilities run in the family."

"You could say that." Lucas favoured her with a small smile.

Jerusha leaned against the table scrutinizing Lucas. "You and Zayna look as if you're growing quite close. You're fitting in quite nicely here. I take it you're happy. You certainly look happier than when you arrived."

"I am," Lucas said. "For the first time in a long while, I feel at peace. And I have you and Zayna to credit for it. I just wish…" he stopped and looked at Jerusha, pondering something.

"What is it? You can tell me anything."

"If Gertrude had written a letter that did not state I was a prince, could you have sent it?"

"I'm sure I could have found a way to send it," Jerusha said after a pause.

Lucas heard the pause and how she had responded, and he couldn't help but frown. He waited a moment and had to ask. "Yes, but *would* you have sent it?"

Jerusha sighed. "I could lie to you and say that I would have. But I just don't know. We've not had to deal with outsiders in years. I'm unsure the council would be comfortable opening the door to communication with your world. I don't think I am. I swore I would be honest with you, and I am."

"Thank you for that." He had known that the answer would be negative. He sighed. "Jerusha, I think Gertrude needs to go home. I have come to believe that I can build a home here, but it's not fair to force her to stay for my sake. She has a family she loves dearly, and she has someone who loves her that she loves back. I saw what happens to a person when they lose someone they love as much as my sister loves Gertrude. I can't keep them apart like this. Can you help her? I haven't seen her since the day you said you spoke with her about her letter. I'm worried."

"You're a good friend, Lucas," Jerusha said. "I will see what I can do. Let me send some people searching for her. It's a small island. She'll be found. Then, I can take your request to the council. If she wishes to leave, we won't keep her here against her will. You aren't our prisoners here after all."

Chapter Sixteen
The Diary

Much to her surprise, Audrina found much comfort in Salazar's company. She found that they had quite a bit in common and found in him an easy listener and a good conversationalist. In her, Salazar found a sympathetic ear, and someone who understood what he was dealing with in his parents, and his situation. It was the first time in his life that he'd found that.

That afternoon, Audrina and Salazar sat together at a large wooden table in King Parven's library. Gwendolyn was accompanying them under the guise of being their chaperone. They had decided that they would play the parts of two young people who were falling for one another. Audrina knew that her grandmother saw right through her guise, but at the same time, she didn't care. So long as her grandfather and Salazar's parents remained in the dark, she was happy with how things were going. Currently, Salazar was helping her go over maps of the area, specifically the largely uncharted area to the east. The more Audrina thought about it, the more she was convinced that this was where Lucas and Gertrude had gone.

"There is quite a bit written about this area," Salazar said regarding the map with a critical eye. "Although most historians disregard it. They find the writings as being written by fanciful drunks and lunatics."

"You don't think so," Gwendolyn said. "I've found in my days as a hedgewitch that the most valuable writings and advice I've come across has usually come from those that the so-called scholars disregard."

Salazar smiled. He nodded. The hedgewitch seemed to understand what he was getting at. "I've brought some of my favourite writings with me." He blushed. "I anticipated being bored while on this trip, so I packed some things to read to pass the time." He indicated a small pile of books that he'd placed on the table by the map. He plucked one from the top. "This one in particular is fascinating. It's a diary written by a merchant sailor named Nico. He says that this area here is one that seems cursed." He indicated the area that Audrina wanted searched. "He says it's more than just the rocks and reefs that causes ships to disappear."

"What is it?" Audrina asked. She leaned over and stared at the map, as if by looking harder, she could will it to offer up its secrets.

"He writes how the waters there teem with mermaids. How their colours make everything glitter like rainbows. But he also talks of a legendary island. Now, everyone scoffs at the stories and declares them impossible."

Audrina stared at Salazar with interest. "What kind of island?"

"According to Nico, this island is one where once you go, you can never return. The people there are isolationist to the extreme. They have found a way to live off magic, where they have no need of the outside world. They are considered to be mystics." Salazar flipped through Nico's diary. "If you look through every kingdom's writings, I mean, go far enough into the history, they all mention an island kingdom with blue-haired kings and queens. And then, all of a sudden, poof!" He made a gesture, as if mimicking an explosion. "It's as if the island never existed.

"Now, an island ruled by a powerful monarchy can't just disappear like that. But, what's interesting is how not too long after the last mention of any trade or treaty with this kingdom, the first blue-haired king turned up, establishing a kingdom just outside of Colonodona." He looked up at Audrina. "It's fascinating that you are convinced that your brother is here. Especially since I think that here," he pointed to the spot on the map, "is exactly where you and your family may have come from."

Audrina felt a shiver crawl up her spine. "And no one believes that these stories are real?"

"Very few do," he said. "Over time, this island has become almost like a ghost story. The mysterious place of kings and queens that just faded from the histories. But I think that every story, every legend has at the very least a kernel of truth to it."

Gwendolyn regarded the map with interest. "What I would like to know is why people don't return. What happens to them on this island?"

"That's just it," Salazar answered. "There's no real way of knowing. If no one comes back, how can we find out what's happening out there."

"How can we go?" Audrina asked. Finally, it felt as if there was a real lead. Maybe now she could have true hope that her brother and Gertrude could come home.

"Go?" Salazar scratched his head, pondering the problem. "Well, we couldn't go in one of the large royal vessels your grandfather favours so much. We would need a much smaller craft. One that could be sailed by one man or two. Then, we could make it past the reefs and rocks a lot easier."

"We?" Gwendolyn asked, eyebrows raised.

"Yes, we." Audrina was firm in her resolve. She was bitter that she had stayed behind when the search had first begun. After all, going by ship to search the waters was not something princesses did. And so, she waited by the docks, she searched the shore. She would not be doing that anymore.

"I highly doubt King Parven would allow you to do this," Gwendolyn said. "Nor you, Audrina. He'd consider it too great a risk for the royal heir of Colonodona. But I could go."

Audrina fumed. She knew Gwendolyn was right. But at the same time, she felt she should do this. Once again, tethered to her duty.

"Hold on, Duchess Gwendolyn," Salazar broke in with a frown. "The princess told me that Queen Sitnalta and King Navor left her here in charge of the search for the prince and your daughter. Her coming on this voyage would be well within the scope of her duty to her mother and father."

Audrina swelled with affection for her new friend. "Thank you, Salazar."

Gwendolyn laughed. "I'm not arguing your logic in this, Salazar, Audrina. I just hope you both realize that you will be in for a fight."

"I do." Audrina was willing to battle this out if she had to.

"Alright then." Gwendolyn looked at the map once more, mentally preparing herself for a sea voyage. "I'll help you fight this on one condition."

Audrina grinned. "Name it."

"You take me with you." She stuck her finger on the map, pointing out the region in the east. "If my daughter is there, I'm going with you to find her."

"I can't deny you this," Audrina said, acquiescing to her demand. "As soon as we're able to go, you will be onboard."

"Agreed." Salazar nodded as he spoke. "If it helps appease your grandparents, I am a skilled sailor, and I am quite knowledgeable when it comes to the region we will be exploring."

Audrina sighed. "I doubt it will help. But if we convince them that we are going out to sea with our faithful chaperone…"

Salazar laughed long and loud. "Oh! My darling princess. Will you accompany me on a romantic search mission? Let us woo one another while we look for your missing brother and true love."

Audrina smacked him in the arm. But she was laughing as well. "Let those busybodies believe what they want. If it helps us get our way, even better."

"When do you think we can depart?" Gwendolyn asked.

"Provided we get our supplies together, I can be prepared to go this evening." Salazar set to work rolling up the maps and gathering his books.

"However, I think that we'd be better served with more daylight. Tomorrow morning; this would also give you time to tell your grandfather our plans. We all know it would be easiest to have the king on our side agreeing to this."

Audrina nodded. This she could do. Pushing herself away from the table, she went off in search of the king.

* * *

Zayna was bewildered. She had told Lucas that she could find Gertrude. Coralnoss was not a big island, and the people on would notice one of the newcomers wandering around. And yet, no one had seen her. It was as if Gertrude had just up and vanished without a trace. Zayna just couldn't understand it. Everywhere she looked she found nothing. Gertrude had not been seen by a single soul since the day she had spoken with Jerusha. If her instincts were correct, Jerusha had been the last person to see Lucas' friend.

Zayna frowned as she stood on the beach. Weeks ago, she had found Lucas and Gertrude on that very spot. Every day she had given thanks that Lucas had come into her life. He was so much lighter and happier than the scared, sad, nervous boy he had been when she had found him. In contrast, it felt as if she had watched Gertrude slide deeper and deeper into herself and her sadness. Looking out at the darkening waves, Zayna got a sick feeling. It seemed as if Gertrude had fallen off the face of the world. What if she had? Zayna got a chill and wrapped her arms around herself, not liking the dark turn her thoughts had taken. But the truth of the matter was that she didn't know what else could have possibly happened. She would have to tell Lucas that she had failed.

Zayna walked into the dining hall and managed a small smile when she saw Lucas sitting with her father. She took a deep breath and walked towards them. Her smile grew a fraction when she heard Lucas call her name. Hearing his voice caused her stomach to flip. She couldn't imagine her life without him now. It was clear that she was falling for him. And now, she feared she was about to hurt him deeply.

"Sit with us," Lucas said.

Zayna nodded and took a seat next to Lucas, across from her father.

"I missed you today," Marcus said. "What were you up to?"

Here it was. She took a deep breath. "I was searching the island for Gertrude. I thought maybe I could figure out what happened."

"And did you?" Marcus had been worried about Gertrude. He'd enjoyed the time they had spent together. The young woman had been knowledgeable and confident, and he'd found her an asset in his work. The people they'd helped together had been calmed by her manner and had found her friendly and personable. And then, she'd vanished.

"That's the thing," Zayna said. She turned to Lucas, prepared to dash his hopes. "I couldn't find her."

"Nowhere?" Marcus asked.

"Nowhere. She might as well have never existed. It's so strange. Father, you know the people of our island."

"I do. They love gossip, and they always will talk about what they've seen, heard, anything. And you, Lucas, you and your friend have been the talk of Coralnoss."

"Exactly." Zayna reached out and took Lucas' hand in hers. "But they have seen nothing, and they're telling me nothing. She hasn't been seen by anyone since the day you told me she went to confront Jerusha about her letter. I don't know what happened to her, but it's becoming more and more clear that she's not on the island."

Marcus frowned, and Lucas narrowed his eyes at Zayna. "What are you saying?" Lucas said.

"I'm saying that I have a very bad feeling. You and I both know that she's been very down this past little while. You were telling me that you thought we should find a way to send her back to Colonodona." She steeled herself for what she knew was coming next.

"So, you think she left, to try to find her way home?" Lucas asked. He thought he could tell what she was trying to say, and he clung to the hope that there might still be a happy ending.

"I wish that were the case." Zayna felt her heart breaking for him. "But there are no boats missing anywhere on the island. Even what's left of yours is still here. The only thing that isn't here is Gertrude."

"So…what does this mean?" Lucas' voice came out in a croak. He didn't want this to be happening.

"I'm not sure," Zayna whispered.

"Yes, you are. Say it. You think, what? What do you think she did? Throw herself into the sea? Do you think she's dead? She harmed herself in some way?" Lucas heard his voice rising and he saw people at the other tables looking their way. He saw them whispering to one another about what they were hearing, but he couldn't bring himself to care.

"No!" Zayna protested. She winced as she said it, realizing that Lucas would know she was being false.

"You are," he said, struggling to keep his voice level.

"I don't want to say it or even think it," Zayna said. "I just… Lucas, you know how she's been since she arrived here. You could see her retreating inwards. She was not happy. You fit in so well, and then we… What did she have? She was not well. Is not well," she hastily corrected. "I just don't know what else could have happened."

Marcus had been sitting and listening to the entire exchange. He had latched on to the information that Gertrude had last been seen speaking with Jerusha, and this was what he clung to. But this could not be spoken about in such a public setting. He rose abruptly from the table. "Come with me," he said in a low voice.

Confused, Lucas and Zayna both rose and followed Marcus out of the dining hall and out of the council building. He led them to the small hut he shared with Zayna in the heart of the town. Lucas and Zayna sat down on two flat cushions as Marcus lit a driftwood fire in his stone hearth. Once the flames crackled, he sat back and let the warmth sink into the room.

"Father?" Zayna said, breaking the silence. "What's going on?"

"Jerusha," he muttered. "You said she was last seen speaking with Jerusha."

"I did."

Marcus leaned forward and put his head in his hands. He took a breath before speaking. "What I'm about to say is merely conjecture. When my daughter said that the people of this island love gossip, she wasn't kidding. For the most part, the stories we tell each other are based in fact. However, some stories are too old, or too odd to be sure anymore.

"Jerusha was once married. Her husband was a fisherman who had a fondness for the drink. He had a reputation of having a nasty temper, one that he took out on his wife whenever she angered him, and being a strong independent woman with a talent for magic, it seemed to happen a lot. Over time, it became clear that she tired of his ill treatment of her, and one night he never came home from his work on the sea. No one has ever outright said that she had a hand in it, but people's suspicions are that she was responsible for her husband's death. No one blames her for it, and many say they would have done the same in her position, but it also is plain that this is largely why she has never had the votes to become chief of the council. She has the experience and the mind for it, but not the trust."

Lucas stared at Marcus in disbelief. "This is merely conjecture. She would never harm Gertrude. An abusive man is hardly the same as a young woman who misses her home."

"True," Marcus conceded. "If it were only her husband, I would gladly agree with you. But there have been other stories. A woman who has concerns over Jerusha's decrees suddenly finds her livestock stricken ill. A man who hurts his wife is mysteriously drowned. Another councilman says something ill-advised about her behind her back and the next day he has a heart attack." He steeled himself for what he had to say next. "I…Zayna, your mother, you know how she was her last days. I

112

told you as much. But what you don't know is she had taken to confiding in Jerusha, and then she…she drowned herself. The only thing I don't understand is what Gertrude could have done to go against her."

Zayna's eyes widened at these revelations. She tried to push her feelings aside and turned to Lucas who nodded. "It was Lucas," she said. "The letter Gertrude wanted Jerusha's help in sending mentioned something about him that would have turned Finn against him."

"And Jerusha is not the type to take losing her new apprentice kindly," Marcus murmured. "She could not have done anything against Finn, so get rid of the one who would cause the problem in the first place." He frowned and looked at Lucas with narrowed eyes. "What was it that she knew?"

Lucas grabbed Zayna's hand for support. He knew this would come up eventually. "It mentioned that I am a prince." He was scared to meet Marcus' eyes. "My mother and father are the queen and king of Colonodona."

"I see." Marcus looked at Lucas with a newfound understanding. He saw the way his daughter looked at him, and as much as he wanted to disapprove, he couldn't find a valid reason as to why he should. Lucas seemed to be the opposite of what he expected a prince to be. The boy seemed content to abandon his birthright for a life that brought him joy. He appeared to have no desire for the trappings of a royal life, and he wanted to do good in this world.

"Father?" Zayna was trying to read her father and see what he was thinking.

"This would indeed cause Finn great disturbance." Marcus sighed. "Lucas, your secret is safe here."

"Thank you." Lucas let out a breath he hadn't realized he'd been holding. "Marcus, if what you say is accurate, then what would Jerusha have done to Gertrude?" He didn't want to think of his teacher as being capable of harming his friend. The very thought gave him a sick feeling. Once again, he'd been duped by someone he'd thought he could trust. Why was he so naïve?

"I don't know," Marcus admitted. "Nothing has ever been proven. It's all been based on coincidences and feelings about her. If, and I say *if*, she did anything, it would not be something that could be traced back to her. What do we know about the last time Gertrude was seen?"

"I know what Lucas told me," Zayna said. "He said that he had told her that Jerusha would not have sent her letter home. Gertrude desperately wanted her parents to know that she was alright. That letter was, in her mind, a lifeline to her parents. She didn't take kindly to the information that it hadn't gone anywhere, and so she went to confront Jerusha."

"After that," Lucas continued for her, "Jerusha told me that Gertrude had, in fact, gone to see her. She said that Gertrude had been upset, and that she had made her a cup of tea to calm her down. Jerusha told me that Gertrude had reacted badly, smashed the cup, and then run from the room. That was the last anyone had seen of her."

Marcus sat up straighter. "She smashed the cup? Wasn't this the day you injured your foot?"

"It was."

"How is it feeling?"

Lucas frowned. Marcus seemed agitated by something. "It still hurts," he admitted. "I can walk on it, but it stings still."

"It shouldn't." Marcus reached for Lucas' leg and took his foot in his lap. He examined the mark on the sole of Lucas' foot with care. It still looked red and slightly inflamed. "You cared for it as I told you to?"

"I did. I stayed off of it as long as you said I should. I elevated it and kept the dressing clean. Why?"

"This should have healed far more than it has. Something got into the wound. I cleaned it before I stitched it, but something is wrong." Marcus put Lucas' foot down. There wasn't anything he could do about it at this stage. "What was it you stepped on?"

"A shard from a smashed cup," Lucas felt the heat in the hit oppressing him. His pulse raced.

"Gertrude's cup?"

Lucas felt Zayna's hand tighten around his. "That is what Jerusha told me."

"If it was merely tea, I don't think it would have affected your wound in this way," Marcus said slowly. "There was something else in that cup. Something that got into your wound. This is bad."

"Poison?" Zayna whispered.

"Not necessarily," Marcus said.

Lucas felt his throat constrict. The world seemed to tilt underneath him. "She killed Gertrude?" he said. He feared knowing the answer.

"I can't say for certain, but it does not look good." Marcus rose and started pacing. "I'm going out tonight. I'm going to see what I can find out." He saw his daughter open her mouth to protest, but he shook his head. "I won't do anything reckless. Trust me, Zayna. I'll return by morning. You two can stay here. I'll be fine."

Marcus bent and kissed Zayna on the top of her head. "We'll talk later."

Lucas and Zayna watched Marcus leave them. Lucas sighed and leaned against Zayna's shoulder. "If anything happened to her, I'll never forgive myself. It's my fault she came here in the first place."

"You need to stop that," Zayna admonished him.

"Stop what?"

"Stop blaming yourself for every decision other people make. You don't control everyone's actions. You didn't force Gertrude onto your boat. You didn't make her fall in love with your sister. You did not kill your former teacher. The only person you control is you."

"I—"

Zayna silenced him with a kiss. She pulled away. "Lucas, I need you to listen to me. Did you grab Gertrude and pull her onto your boat?" He shook his head. "Did you force her to stay on board as you sailed here? Make her write a letter? Lock her in a room with Jerusha and argue with her?"

"No."

"The only thing you did is decide to run away from home. That part is on you. The rest is Gertrude's choice. Blaming yourself will not help her or save her. It will only render you upset, and you upset is not useful."

Lucas sighed. "You're right." He looked around the hut, taking in the ingredients drying from the rafters for use in potions and remedies. He looked at the cozy fire crackling in the hearth, and he turned and saw the sleeping area just around a corner. His face flushed as he looked back into Zayna's shining face. "How long will your father be?"

"He may be a good long while," she said with a coy smile.

"Hmmm." Lucas pulled Zayna closer until she was almost seated in his lap. He traced a finger up her arm and hooked it under the strap of her dress. She reached up and helped him undo it.

"A good, long while," she whispered and leaned down to kiss him again. She could think of a few things they could do to pass the time.

Lucas allowed himself to be distracted. He needed some more good memories. He had a feeling his happiness would be fleeting.

Chapter Seventeen
Departures

"No." King Parven's face was red with anger. "I cannot, I *will* not allow this. You are a princess. You are the heir to a throne." He broke off, feeling anxious as to where this conversation was going. He felt a lump well up in his throat. "Audrina, please. I have already lost one of my grandchildren. I have no intention of losing another."

Audrina crossed her arms over her chest and glared at her grandfather. The conversation was going about as well as she'd predicted it would: terribly. She had tried to reason with him. She had tried begging. She had tried bargaining. But nothing seemed to be working. She understood how he felt, but she also knew what had to be done.

"Grandfather," she began again. She fought to keep her voice level. "I've already told you that my parents tasked me with—"

"I don't care what you have convinced yourself your duty is," Parven growled. He was growing evermore frustrated with the conversation. The girl just wouldn't see reason! "Your duty to your kingdom supersedes all of that. If you were to drown out there or disappear like your brother…" He broke off mid-sentence. He wasn't really sure why. The thought of losing both of his grandchildren brought him up short. He knew that was something he just couldn't handle. Thinking of his son losing all of his children stopped him from speaking momentarily. He shut his eyes and took a breath.

Audrina pressed her lips together. Seeing the pain on her grandfather's face made her rethink all that had been said. It was clear that this was about more than just duty. "Grandfather," she said, softening her tone. "I'm not doing this alone. I'm going with Salazar. His parents have assured me he is a skilled sailor, and he understands where we're headed. Gwendolyn is accompanying us as well. Her skill as a healer, while hopefully unnecessary, will be useful, and she wants to find her daughter."

"Audrina," Parven sighed. "Your hope that your brother is still alive, while admirable, I have to ask…"

"He is alive." Audrina spoke with conviction. "They both are. I can't lose them."

Parven's eyes narrowed a fraction. He had heard her speak of the duke's daughter frequently. He saw that there was a lot of affection between the girls. He heard it in his granddaughter's words. But there was something more there, and it gave him pause. "Them?" Parven said.

"Yes. Them." Audrina felt a twinge of nerves. Parven's mood had shifted and she was unsure of what caused it.

"It seems that you've put equal importance on your friend and brother," Parven said. "Why is that?"

"I—" Audrina didn't know what to say to this. "How should I act? Should I not care that she's missing? Should I not care that Ipsinki and Gwendolyn's daughter is gone? She is their only child, after all."

"I didn't say that."

"No, but you insinuated as much." Audrina was frustrated and angry. "I care Lucas is gone. I care very deeply. Do you want to know how I really feel? I feel responsible. I feel that this is my fault. My fault because I didn't do enough to help him after everything that happened back home. I didn't act as if I cared. I could have been a better sister. I could have been better for him." The words started pouring out of her in a rush. She had had enough, enough of people telling her what to do, enough of being told how to feel and what her future was.

"Audrina, I understand, but that does not excuse your rushing off on a whim."

"A whim? I have been patient and obedient. I have waited for your men to go and find them, and nothing has happened. I have a plan, a plan that I believe will work. And I am executing it. With or without your permission."

"I will not allow it," Parven said, a threatening note in his voice.

"With all due respect, I no longer care what you allow." Audrina saw Parven's face fill with anger and disbelief.

"How dare you?" Parven ground out.

"I dare quite a bit," Audrina said. "And as for Gertrude," Audrina was shaking as she looked into her grandfather's eyes. "I love her. I have loved her for years. I love her the way my mother loves my father. And no matter how many high-born men you and my grandmother want to flaunt in front of me, I will never choose one of them. Gertrude is the one who has my heart."

Parven was apoplectic. "Degenerate!" he gasped. "This is madness! How can my granddaughter, the heir to the throne choose such a life? It is your duty to provide a future for your kingdom! Think of it! A childless life, choosing love over your people. This is madness! No one else has done what you propose. And you do this for *both* our kingdoms? A rule with no successor, the people against you, against *me* for allowing it? I cannot. I *will* not!"

"I didn't choose," Audrina cried. "I am the way I am. It's how I've always been. I'm sorry you don't understand. But I am going. I am going with Salazar and with Gwendolyn to find my brother and the one I love."

"Go," King Parven growled. "Get out of my sight."

Audrina turned and ran from the room. Parven sat shaking with anger. He seethed over his granddaughter's words and eventually stood and began to pace. He didn't know what to say or think. A princess making such a choice. She was a disgrace. He would not abide it. He couldn't.

Kika entered the room, her soft footsteps causing him to turn. She shook her head. "Parven, I saw our granddaughter running towards the docks. She was crying. What happened?"

"No. Not our granddaughter," Parven grit out.

Kika felt her throat constrict. "What are you saying?"

"Did you know about her infatuation with the duke's daughter?" Parven asked.

"I did," Kika admitted. She flinched at the look her husband gave her. "I haven't known for long. She told me about it and I assumed it was something that we could convince her to ignore. That she would do what was right as a princess."

"This is because of her father. It has to be." Parven resumed his pacing, ranting with every step.

"What do you mean?" Kika felt a chill as she watched Parven. Her husband appeared to have lost his mind. She'd never seen him act this way before.

"How can you ask that?" Parven demanded. "He's not our son! Remember? How he told us how he came to be? How he was merely a product of that coin. So of course his children would be deviants! One of them practices the type of magic that nearly ruined this family. And her! What are we going to do about this?"

Kika stared at her husband as if he were a stranger. "How can you say this? You love our son, just as I do. And maybe Audrina may be making a choice that we don't agree with, but she is our granddaughter. We've lost our grandson. Please don't drive her away as well. This is my family. *Our* family. I can't lose my child and my grandchildren over this. Please." She stared at her husband, tears in her eyes. He looked at her as though she had lost her mind.

"How else could this have happened?" Parven asked. "We have gone centuries ruling this island without such things happening in our history. And now, our son, coming to us the way he did, and both of his children… Misfits. Oddities. How else could this have happened? They will lead hard lives. The boy, Lucas, I understand he did not choose. But her?"

Kika frowned at her husband. "I don't believe she chose either," she said softly. "You are being cruel, Parven. And cruelty doesn't become you. You saw how your words wounded that girl. Knowing her as we do, loving her, as we have. Think on this before you drive your family away from you."

"You mean from 'us,'" Parven retorted.

"No, I don't," Kika replied. "I meant what I said, exactly as I said it. I will not lose my family over this. Whether or not you do…that is a choice you have to make for yourself."

Parven breathed heavily, staring at his wife in shock. "Ultimately, I am the king," he said. "I have to do what's best for my people. A queen such as she will be is not that. Get her betrothed to that boy, Salazar," he growled. "She will not humiliate us with this nonsense. Make her see reason, and I will forget today ever happened."

"I will try," Kika whispered, and she fled from the room in search of her granddaughter, hoping it wasn't too late.

Kika finally caught up with Audrina. She was standing on the dock saying her goodbyes to Gerald.

"Audrina," Kika called. "Please wait."

Audrina looked up at her grandmother, she felt wounded, unsure of herself. "What do you want?" Audrina asked.

"Please be safe," Kika said. "When you're out there. Find Gertrude and find your brother and come home safely."

Audrina stared at her grandmother, trying to see if this was a trap. "Did you speak to King Parven?"

Kika was disappointed by Audrina not calling the king "grandfather" as she usually did. "I did," she said. "But I need you to know that I don't feel as he does. Give him time. I love you." Kika pulled Audrina in and hugged her tight.

"Thank you," Audrina whispered. "That means a lot."

"Bring them home," Kika said.

"We will." Audrina turned and hopped onto the boat where Gwendolyn and Salazar were waiting. They pulled up anchor and Salazar steered them out of the cove and out to open sea.

On the dock, Kika stood at Gerald's side watching as the small craft shrank away from view. Gerald looked over where Kika stood. She still looked upset and bothered.

"What else did your husband say?" Gerald asked in an undertone.

Kika sighed. "We both want what's best for that girl," she said. "Am I right in believing that about you?"

"I love these children as if they truly were my grandchildren. You know I raised her mother as best I could. Aud and I both did. Aud did from birth." Gerald looked misty at the mention of the late queen.

"I know." Kika stood, still watching the horizon. "Parven said he would forgive her if she agrees to the betrothal with Salazar."

Gerald scoffed. "Forgive? What is there to forgive? She loves who she loves. The truth is that there is nothing wrong with the princess. In all my years, political marriages, betrothals in exchange for treaties, and alliances through selling our children have very seldom ended in happy marriages. Did you know that I met Sitnalta through Supmylo trying to arrange a marriage between she and I?"

"That's absurd."

"Any more absurd than Audrina declaring she loves Gertrude?" Gerald raised his eyebrows at Kika. "Parven is angry because this is something that, to him at least, feels outside his scope of understanding. Forcing his granddaughter to marry will not change who she is, but it will end with her miserable. You cannot honestly tell me this is something you want for her. I understand he has some say, as she will rule here as well, but this is too much. It is unfair of him."

"I married for an alliance," Kika said. "I love my husband, and I have been happy. I am also not naïve. I realize that my marriage is not usual in this regard. But Salazar is a good man. I know him, and I know his parents. He will do what he can to make Audrina happy. Look at what he's doing for her now." She gestured to the waves.

"I know you mean well," Gerald said. "I understand this. I really do. But this has to be Audrina's choice. This can't be something that she feels pushed or forced into. If she is, she will never truly be happy, and how can someone who feels trapped run a kingdom at its best?"

Kika smiled softly at Gerald. "Aud was a lucky woman."

"I was the lucky one," he whispered. "I don't know I ever truly realized how lucky until she was gone."

"The children are lucky to have you." Kika watched the lines of his face in the sun. She wished she had his strength and wisdom.

"And you," Gerald said. "It can't be easy to disagree with a man like your husband."

Kika shook her head. "I will do my best for Audrina," she vowed.

"And I will stand by you." Gerald offered his arm to the queen, and together they walked back to the castle.

* * *

Lucas woke up surrounded by warmth and soft hands holding him close. It took him a moment to recognize where he was. He had fallen asleep in Zayna's arms in the hut she shared with her father. At the thought of Marcus, Lucas sat up quickly and looked around. The healer wasn't there, and it was still dark outside. He could just see the faintest hint of a lightening sky outside the window. It appeared as if Marcus had not returned home. Beside him, Zayna began to stir. She opened sleepy eyes and smiled up at him.

"Is it morning yet?" she asked with a yawn.

"Not quite," Lucas replied.

"Then lie back down with me."

"And if your father comes home and finds us like this?" Lucas did not want to think about such a thing happening. He didn't think he could talk his way out of that situation.

Zayna hummed as she thought it over. "I think we can make him see reason. But you're probably right." She rose, and the blanket fell from her shoulders, offering Lucas a view of her that drove the blood from his face. He watched as she fetched a night shirt from a low chest and slipped it over her head.

"Where are you going?" He watched as she wandered through the hut, picking up a copper kettle and filling it from a barrel of water.

"Are you hungry?" She set the kettle over the fire and grabbed a couple of plates.

"Famished." Lucas climbed out of bed and dressed quickly. He joined her in front of the fire, and the two of them worked quickly to prepare a small breakfast. Soon they were sitting together in comfortable silence eating a simple meal of eggs and fruit and sipping honeyed tea.

"I'm concerned that Father didn't return home last night, Zayna said with a frown as she cleared the plates. "While it's nice we weren't interrupted, I don't know what could have waylaid him. It's been hours. I wish I knew what was happening."

Lucas rose to help her wash them off. Together, up to their elbows in fire-warmed water they washed the dishes, both filled with worry for the people they were missing.

"Your father is a smart man," Lucas assured her. "Perhaps he just got waylaid following a lead. I'm sure he'll be back."

"I hope so." Zayna lapsed back into silence and put their plates away. "I'm going to go and get dressed." She raised herself up and kissed Lucas before turning to go and pull on her clothes.

Lucas settled back in front of the fire and tried to relax. A knock sounded on the door. He rose to answer it thinking it might be an islander looking for their healer to help them with some problem. Instead, he found himself face-to-face with the pink-haired merchant he'd met the first day he'd wandered the island.

"Mott!" Lucas exclaimed upon seeing him.

"Hello," Mott said with a small smile.

"Can I help you? Are you looking for Marcus?"

"Actually, Marcus sent me here to see you and his daughter." Mott shrugged. "I came to deliver a message."

"Alright. What is it?" Lucas felt relieved. If Mott had come with a message for them, then surely he was still alright and everything would be fine.

Mott handed Lucas a folded-up piece of parchment that had been sealed shut with a gob of wax. "Marcus is in the council building. Or, at least he was when I last saw him. Well, good day, Lucas!"

"Good day, Mott. Thank you for the message." Lucas watched Mott amble off down the road and shut the door. He turned around to see Zayna standing there, dressed in a flowing green dress and her hair tied back in a long braid.

"Who was that?"

"It was Mott, the fruit seller. He came with a message from your father. He said he saw Marcus in the council building."

"So, what does the message say?" Zayna eyed the parchment with interest.

"I haven't read it yet." Lucas cracked the seal and unfolded the note. He sat down with Zayna at his side, and they read it together.

Zayna,

> *I have found someone who says that they know where I can find our lost friend. They say they saw what happened to her. I am meeting with him at dawn. Until then, I will see what else I can find out. But what I am certain of is that she's alive. Or at least she was after her talk with the person we were discussing. So we will cling to that hope. Tell our boy that we will find her. I have faith that this will work out. Somehow.*

Your father

"He didn't mention anyone by name," Lucas said with a frown. The style of writing didn't gel with what he knew of the healer. It seemed off somehow.

"Of course he didn't," Zayna replied. "If Jerusha got a hold of this, he had to give himself plausible deniability. This way he gave no indication that we suspect her of anything."

"I suppose." Lucas read the letter over another couple of times. "But she's alive." Lucas allowed himself to feel hope. If Marcus was hopeful, he could be too.

"Yes. She's alive." Zayna leaned against Lucas. "When we find her, will you help her get off the island?"

Lucas nodded. "She wants to go home. I care about her. How can I call myself her friend, and keep her from her family and the one she loves? I can't do that."

"But what about you? Will you go with her?" Zayna looked into Lucas' eyes fearing the answer.

"How can I leave?" Lucas said. He held Zayna close. "I love you." He had said it without thinking, and he knew it to be true. He just hoped she felt the same.

Zayna smiled. She felt warmed by his words. "I love you, too."

He leaned in and kissed her. "I would never leave you. My home is here now. With you. I will help Gertrude get to her home, and I will stay here."

Chapter Eighteen
Landing

Gertrude sat in the dark. The room she was in had no windows, and the door was kept locked and barred. Every so often, someone unseen slipped a tray of barely edible food through a small flap in the bottom of the door. The first few times it had happened, Gertrude had cried out to them, trying to figure out anything: where she was, who was out there, what time it was, even how long she had been there. But the response was always silence. Occasionally, her ears pricked with the sound of scuttling feet scurrying across the stone floor. In one corner of her cell, Gertrude had found a bucket. Other than that, she had been left alone.

When she was able to sleep, her dreams were plagued with visions of Audrina. She was a spectre at the princess' wedding to some noble stranger. She was an unseen ghoul, haunting Audrina from afar, watching as the princess was forced to live a life she did not want. Other dreams had her watch as Lucas was trapped on this island, living under Jerusha's thumb. Though she knew he claimed to love it here, how could she live her life in the dark, knowing that he was spending his time with the woman who had drugged her and left her to this fate?

Gertrude shuddered as she sat with her knees drawn up to her chest, her arms hugging them close to her body. The scuttling sounds were back. Whatever creatures she shared this dank prison with, they were prowling around in the dark now, looking for some scraps of food, or someway to see what she was made of. Gertrude suppressed a sob. She didn't know if there were any guards out in the hall beyond her door, but she wouldn't give them the satisfaction of hearing her cry. She wouldn't let on how she'd been broken by her isolation.

In spite of her best efforts, tears slid down her cheeks. She sniffed quietly as she let the darkness close in on her like a blanket. It was all she saw, all she felt. What she wouldn't give for one more glance at Audrina's smiling face, one more time of hearing her name fall from the princess' lips, one more time to feel Audrina's arms around her. But these were things Gertrude knew she could never have. Hope had died there in that cell. Now Gertrude waited for her turn to die with it.

* * *

Marcus frowned, driving the lines at the sides of his mouth deeper into his cheeks. Nothing seemed right. In his gut, he felt that Gertrude still lived. The fact that he couldn't find a trace of her anywhere didn't make a lick of sense to him. He prowled the main foyer of the council building waiting. He'd heard that some of the council's guards had watched as an unconscious Gertrude had been taken from Jerusha's study. Unconscious. He clung to that word with all he had. He had been honest with Lucas. He had liked Gertrude. There had been something in her sad, sweet nature that had reminded him of his late wife. When Gertrude had disappeared, he had feared the worst. He had seen the same look in her eyes that he had seen in the eyes of Zayna's mother. The same quiet determination. But with his wife, she had gone for a walk one day, leaving him with their little girl. She had gone for a walk and been found hours later, nestled in the rocks at low tide. He had feared that Gertrude had come to the same fate, and that once again, he had seen it and done nothing.

But, after speaking with Lucas, he knew that this time, he could save her. This time, things were different, and everything pointed to Jerusha. And so, he waited. He would speak with the council guards, and he would find his apprentice. He heard the heavy footsteps approaching and he turned, eyes widening in surprise.

"Chief Councilman," Marcus said with an inclining of his head.

"Marcus. What brings you here at this hour?" Finn looked at Marcus with a suspicious glint in his eye.

"I was looking for my new apprentice, Gertrude. I'd been told that someone here might know of her whereabouts." Marcus looked Finn over carefully. He wondered if there was anyone on the council who might be considered trustworthy. He doubted there would be any way to truly find out.

"I see." Finn's eyes narrowed minutely. "I've heard a few things. I'd like to compare notes, if you're up to it. Follow me."

Marcus didn't see what choice he had. He followed Marcus through the spiralling corridor towards the main council chamber. Marcus watched, heart thumping in his chest as Finn unlocked the door and led him through. His spirit sank. He should have known it wouldn't be so easy. Finn led him towards the truth stone and turned to face him.

"I'll tell you what I know, if you tell me what you do," Finn said, his voice even and calm.

"You first," Marcus said. He knew that he was pushing the chief, but he was feeling reckless. Something rotten was happening in Coralnoss. He didn't know to what extent, or even who was in on it. But he was getting tired of being deferential.

Finn heard the challenge in Marcus' voice. Something in it intrigued him. Here was someone strong. He could use people like this on the council at his side. Truth be told, he was getting tired of people kowtowing to him and leaving the judgements squarely on his shoulders. He could use a good challenge.

"Alright, Marcus," Finn said. "The stone is here. We both know that I cannot lie to you. I have been hearing whispers about your apprentice. I allowed both her and Lucas to remain on this island free to live within our laws and our borders. So to hear that she was not happy here after my kindness, and to hear that she disappeared, to say that I was disappointed is an understatement.

"I have my people here in Coralnoss, those who are loyal to me. They have been reporting to me about what's been happening with her. I know that she wrote a letter home. As a father, I can understand her desire to let her parents know that she is alive. I would wish that from my son. If I'd known, if I'd seen that letter I would have found a way to send it."

Marcus looked sharply at the truth stone, but there was no change. He felt a twinge of surprise that the chief was telling the truth.

"I would have sent it," Finn repeated. "Provided there was a way to send it without the recipient finding out where we are, and if there wasn't anything untoward in it. I take no pleasure in knowing that a family believes their child has died. I am not a monster, Marcus, regardless of what some may believe. But I saw no such letter.

"After this incident, I believe is when she was last seen. Unfortunately, here reports get muddled, and I am not happy about it."

"What do you mean 'muddled'?" Marcus asked, voice sharp.

"My power is limited," Finn reluctantly admitted. "While I have those here who are loyal, there are those who may have…other allegiances."

Marcus grunted. He had a hunch he knew who they were loyal to.

"You know something," Finn said.

Marcus knew it was not a request. He had to start talking. "What I know is mostly conjecture at this point," he said. "Quite frankly, some of it is based in rumours."

"We both know that most rumours on this island have their start in truth," Finn flatly pointed out.

Marcus nodded. "There was a letter. Gertrude wrote it and gave it to Lucas. He suspected that she wanted to go home. At the same time, he thought as you do. The girl's parents have a right to know she is safe and well. So, he took the letter and gave it to Jerusha."

Finn took in a sharp breath. This wasn't lost on Marcus. He chose his next words carefully, keeping his eyes on the stone. A lie by omission could not be counted as a true lie by the stone. "What happened next gets slightly confused when it comes to Gertrude. What we do know is that my daughter told Lucas that she didn't believe that Jerusha would send the letter, or even give it to the council. Lucas told this to Gertrude who confronted Jerusha. That was the last she was seen."

"At least by us." Marcus looked at Finn, steadily meeting his eyes. "That day, Jerusha said that she gave Gertrude a calming tea, and that Gertrude responded by smashing the cup on the floor. Lucas stepped on one of the shards. One of the guards here informed me that he saw Gertrude being removed from Jerusha's study unconscious."

Finn swore under his breath upon hearing this. "What are your thoughts on this?"

"I think it has validity. There was something in that cup, something other than tea." Marcus saw how disturbed Finn was about this, but at the same time, he also seemed unsurprised. "Lucas' foot wound is not healing correctly. Tea would not cause this, and he believes that Gertrude is not the type who would harm herself."

"You feared she would?" Finn looked carefully at Marcus and almost missed the slight nod. "I apologize. You would know better than most. Please know that I don't take pleasure in dredging up these painful memories. Your wife was a wonderful woman."

"Thank you." Marcus breathed easier. "You've suspected Jerusha of deception?"

"In some cases. I hate admitting this, and to most people, even members of the council, I would not." Finn was clearly upset. All of this angered him. Marcus could see it simmering under the surface. "Jerusha has eyes, just as I do. We both know that there are those who believe that she should have my seat. I believe that on the next vote, she probably will best me for support, and that is the people's right. If my time as chief is done, I will step down. But I believe that she is sometimes unscrupulous. She has used her powers and knowledge of poisons in the past to harm others."

"Her husband?" Marcus asked.

"You've heard the rumours." Finn began to pace. He was never one for idle gossip. All this itched under his skin. "As I said, in any rumour, there is the kernel of truth at the heart of the story. But I have to believe, as you do, that the girl still lives. Jerusha must need her for something."

"But what?" Marcus asked.

"I don't know. But Marcus, I need to know why Jerusha kept the letter from us." Finn fixed Marcus with a piercing stare. "What was written in the letter?"

Chapter Nineteen
A Time for Truth

Marcus held his breath. He could feel sweat needing on his brow. His eyes flicked to the truth stone. He wondered how big a lie he would have to tell to set it off, and he knew that he didn't want to find out. He thought quickly. "I never read the letter," he said. That was the truth. He knew that the stone would hear it.

Finn smiled grimly. Clever man. Nice try. "Never read it. But you do know what set Jerusha off. Don't you?"

Marcus closed his eyes and grimaced. It seemed he had a choice: tell the truth and betray Lucas and Zayna, or refuse to speak and lose Finn as a potential ally. Gertrude's pale, sad face swam in his memory. He would not lose someone as he lost his wife. He had sworn to his daughter and to Lucas that he would find Gertrude. He needed Finn to do that.

"You are not going to like what I have to say," he said in a low voice. "Please, keep in mind how well Lucas has fit in in our society, of all the good work he has done here."

"Marcus," Finn started. He knew instinctively that whatever the healer was keeping from him would be upsetting.

"You know our history better than most. You know why we keep ourselves apart from those that call themselves 'kingdoms.'" Marcus paused and gathered his thoughts, searching for the right words to convince Finn not to turn against their guests. "We don't choose who we are born to. And Lucas left of his own volition. You know he didn't lie about any of that. However, what he didn't say is who he was born to. What his title was. And this was what Gertrude put in the letter."

Finn cursed under his breath. He should have known! "He's royal," he growled. "After years of keeping that way of life at bay, I let one of them slip into our land. And you knew?"

"I found out today," Marcus said. "But Chief, Lucas is as different from those who were exiled as anyone could be. I know that, and I'm sure your 'eyes' know that as well. He is a good boy."

Finn struggled to regain his composure. Part of him felt he should have thrown that boy to the sharks. But he also saw the truth in Marcus' words. He took a series of calming breaths. "You are right. He left that all behind, and he has joined us wholeheartedly. I just hate feeling deceived."

"We all do," Marcus assured him.

"Thank you for your honesty," Finn said. The traditional ending to a council period of questioning. He wandered the room, mulling over his options. If he knew Jerusha, she would want to keep her new toy. That meant destroying the letter and hiding all who knew of its contents. A young woman like Gertrude would be a good pawn to keep alive. She would guarantee Lucas' cooperation by keeping his friend alive. At the same time, where would she hide someone she didn't want found? He thought over the information he had gathered from his network. Food had been siphoned off and sent off by men who were loyal to her. His eyes narrowed. She had thought she could keep her secrets. But she couldn't keep things from him for long.

"Let me check a few ideas I have," Finn said to Marcus. "We will find her before long. I can promise you that."

"And Jerusha?" Marcus asked.

"Maybe her secrets will cease to be rumours," Finn said with grim satisfaction. Taking her down would guarantee his reelection. He could live with that.

* * *

Audrina was trying her best to be helpful, but as the voyage progressed, it was becoming more and more clear that she was relatively useless. Salazar was acting as if he was born on the deck of a sailing ship and watching him as he gracefully worked the rigging and kept their course she was filled with admiration for her new friend. Gwendolyn was also a natural, her strong, calloused hands knew their way around the ship's rudder, taking Salazar's instructions with an easy understanding that went over the princess' head. So, Audrina had made herself their eyes. As they sailed along the course Salazar had planned for them, Audrina kept her eyes on the water. She scanned the waves, searching for some sign of a boat that sailed sails of her grandparents' kingdom's colours. She searched for any of her brother's belongings bobbing along the surface of the water. She knew that the chances of seeing anything was minuscule at best, but still, she searched.

"Here." Gwendolyn made her way wobbly across the deck to where Audrina sat, perched and staring. She pressed an apple into the princess' hand. "We need to keep our strength up. Eat."

Audrina took the offered fruit. She hadn't realized how much time had passed since she'd last eaten. "Thank you." She gratefully bit into the apple and quickly ate it down to the core. "Have you eaten?"

"I have. And so has Salazar. Let's face it, I've taken the role of the ship's mother. And a mother always makes her children eat." Gwendolyn gave a self-deprecating smile. "How are you holding up?"

"I keep looking out there, half expecting to see some sign of them. But I know, deep down that there will be nothing there." Audrina shrugged and pitched the pips overboard.

"I know the feeling well," Gwendolyn said. She wrapped her arm around Audrina's shoulder. "I have faith in our sea-legged friend. I have a good feeling about our trip. We'll find them."

Audrina gave Gwendolyn a nervous look. "I agree with you that we will find them. That's not what I'm worried about."

Gwendolyn's smile faltered. "What is it? What's bothering you?"

"I'm that obvious?" Audrina gave a short laugh.

"I've known you since the day you were born. I delivered you after all. I can tell when you're upset, and right now, something is bothering you." Gwendolyn gave her an encouraging squeeze.

Audrina paused, hesitant to speak her mind, as if saying it out loud would make her fears manifest and become a reality.

"Grief shared is grief halved," Gwendolyn murmured in her ear. "At least, that's what my mother used to tell me."

"What if they don't want to come home?" Audrina said in a small voice. "What if we find them, and they don't want to come home with us?"

Gwendolyn felt goosebumps prickle over her arms. This was something she had never considered. *Never allowed yourself to consider,* an insidious voice whispered in the back of her mind. She refused to believe that her daughter would turn her back on them, on their family. But then she remembered Gertrude's face at dinner that last night at King Parven's castle.

"You're both looking serious," Salazar called from his position at the stern at the ship. "I don't mean to intrude, but we should be hitting the reefs by night fall. In a few hours, I will need both of your help. I have no intention of capsizing. Do you?"

"I refuse to let you go down that path," Gwendolyn said to Audrina. She turned back to Salazar. "I'll be right there!" She turned back to Audrina. "We'll cross this bridge if and when we come to it. We need to find them first, and then any issues can be dealt with them. I insist on being optimistic."

"I'll try to do the same," Audrina promised. She watched as Gwendolyn ably crossed the ship to receive instruction from Salazar. She turned to look back over the waves.

Chapter Twenty
The Cells

Finn sat at his desk, maps, plans, and papers scattered across the weathered top. If anyone had entered the room they would have found him hopelessly disorganized, but to him, there was an order to the chaos. He had known. There had been rumours of it for years, and yet, he had never wanted to find out for himself. He had an instinctual aversion to anything associated to the old monarchy. Everything else the former king and queen had built, their former splendour had been razed to the ground. And yet, rumours persisted about things that remained. Things that were underneath, underground. He had never gone looking.

But Jerusha had.

That thought stuck in his mind like a bur. *Jerusha had.* The more he went over all these writings, these plans, the more he realized how much more she knew than he did. He hated that. He had to tread lightly now. He couldn't allow himself to show his anger and go off after her. No. He had to slowly discover what she had and make it seem as if he had no knowledge of the councilwoman's interest in Lucas' friend. He had to make it seem as if his only target was Gertrude. But treading lightly had never been his forte. He rose and poured himself a drink. He needed something strong after the long night he had had. He had a feeling it would be the first of many such nights.

Finn threw back the remainder of his drink and rolled up the top city plan. Marcus was the one he knew he could trust with this. If their talk had shown him anything, it showed him this. He needed to speak with Marcus.

* * *

Marcus sat in his hut, his daughter at his side. Lucas sat across from him, and he had to laugh. It was as if the prince was afraid to meet his eyes. Zayna kept trying to get Lucas' attention, but the boy seemed frightened of something. He wasn't an idiot. He knew exactly what had happened while he was absent. He might not like it, but he wouldn't lash out at either of them.

"Father," Zayna said. "What happened last night? I was worried. And then Mott arrived with a note from you. Did you find anything out?"

"I did. I ended up speaking with Finn." Marcus looked from one to the other, and he saw Zayna's eyes widen.

"And?"

Marcus knew this would happen. He knew he could drag it out, but he needed to get it over with, get it all out of the way. He looked over at Lucas. "Lucas, look at me please."

Lucas looked up hesitantly.

"I am so sorry," Marcus said. "I knew that I gave you my word that I would keep your confidence, but some things needed to be said. Finn knows about you."

Zayna gasped. "What is he going to do about this? Father, I will not give him up. We love each other."

Marcus looked into Lucas' eyes, and Lucas nodded. "I love your daughter," the prince said. "My intentions are noble."

Marcus raised an eyebrow at this, and he had to laugh as Lucas turned bright red.

"What does the chief want from me?" Lucas asked. "I don't want to leave."

"Your leaving was never discussed," Marcus assured him. He saw both Lucas and Zayna relax at his words. "I needed to be honest with him to gain his trust. He knows that Jerusha probably did something to Gertrude. We are working together to discover what that was. He has long suspected that the councilwoman was planning something. He stayed behind to do some more research. I hope to hear more today. Hopefully he learned something that can help us."

"So, Chief Finn is on our side?" Zayna said in shock. She couldn't stop the grin from spreading across her face.

"This is good news?" Lucas said. "Somehow I don't see an upside to this. He knows I'm royalty. Everyone on this island hates what I am. If this comes out, how can I show my face around these streets?"

"I believe that it is in Finn's best interest to keep our confidence on this," Marcus said. "He won't say anything. If it gets out that he allowed a royal to stay on this island, and be mentored by a member of the council, it will skewer his chances of being chosen again by the people to lead our council and lead Coralnoss."

"He'll stay quiet about this, Lucas," Zayna said. "If my father says he will, I believe him."

"Okay," Lucas said.

"Marcus!"

Marcus turned at the sound of the voice outside. Chief Councilman Finn was at the door. Marcus hurried to answer the door. He pulled the door open and Finn pushed his way inside. Marcus steered him to a seat by the fire.

"Chief Councilman," Zayna said. "Welcome to our home."

"Chief," Lucas said with a polite nod. He felt nervous having the chief there, knowing who and what he was.

"Zayna, Lucas," Finn said, acknowledging each in turn. He turned to the prince looking him right in the face. He didn't know what he expected to see, and he certainly wasn't prepared for a nervous young man who seemed scared to learn his fate. He knew what his next move needed to be. "Lucas, I know where you come from and what you were. I say were, because here, we have no royalty. You are not a prince. Is that correct?"

"It is," Lucas acknowledged. "But I would go further. If I was to be honest, I believe that I stopped thinking of myself as a prince the day I started learning magic from my old mentor, Kralc."

"Thank you, Lucas." Finn pulled out the plans he had brought. "Now, I understand that we are all in agreement that Jerusha probably had a hand in this. I found several historical tomes had been removed from our archives and placed in her possession, as well as some building plans for the island. I have in my hand a copy of one of these plans." He spread out the plan in question.

"What are we looking at?" Zayna asked as she looked over the spidery handwriting and the drawings in front of her. "It almost looks as if we're looking at the council building. But taller."

"What this is is the old castle. When the rebellion happened, the castle was demolished. The council building was built where the old castle stood." Finn gestured to the drawing. "We thought we had thoroughly buried the old regime. But, as you can see, what was is now lurking under the surface."

Lucas peered at the drawings with interest. He saw immediately what Finn was indicating. "There's something below," he said, pointing. "Dungeons?"

"The old monarchs believed in cruel punishments," Finn said. "Their jail cells were an action in cruelty. No windows, damp walls, no contact with any other human being."

Lucas shuddered. "You think they still exist."

"I do," Finn said. "And furthermore, I believe that Jerusha found them, and that she is using them."

Lucas felt sick. Thinking of Gertrude locked away in such a place was horrifying to him. "How do we find them and get her out?"

"I think I know where they may be," Finn said. "Give me today. By nightfall, hopefully this will all be over."

Lucas watched as the chief rose to leave. "Finn," he said. He looked into his eyes and stood. Lucas stuck out his hand. "Thank you for believing in me. I'm sorry I didn't tell you everything the day we met. I…"

"I understand why you didn't." Finn took the offered hand and squeezed it. "You are a credit to us, Lucas. I will keep your confidence."

Lucas watched him leave. He stood long after the door had closed behind the chief. He allowed himself a small smile as Zayna came to stand by his side.

"Tonight," she whispered. "He said it would be over tonight. Until then, come to the beach with me. Father says he can spare me today. I think he needs his rest."

Lucas saw Marcus stumbling off to bed and nodded. Everyone here had been trying so hard to help. A little sleep was the least he could offer. He murmured a slumbering spell and sent it off in Marcus' direction. His sleep would be restful and his dreams would be peaceful. He deserved that much. Taking Zayna's hand, he let himself be led off in the direction of their beach.

* * *

The sun was setting over the horizon. Audrina watched as the sky became tinged with pinks and purples. She saw something splashing in the water and stared in amazement as a mermaid came into view. She smiled wistfully thinking about how Gertrude would love to see this. She couldn't wait for all this to be over. She looked back, feeling as if there was something she should be contributing. Both Salazar and Gwendolyn were focusing on steering them through the rocks and coral that could be seen just under the water's surface. Audrina could see the brightly coloured coral formations below them. Here and there, rainbow fish flitted through openings and hiding in small holes. She saw more mermaids swimming under the water. Their dark shapes striking easily through the currents below, their strong tails propelling them forward.

"We should get there soon," Salazar called to her. "Keep a lookout for land."

"I will," Audrina called back. She could feel the wind picking up around them, and the waves kicked up a salt spray that misted her face. She took his instruction seriously, scanning the darkening sky intently. She would not steer them wrong. A crunch, followed by their boat lurching to the side nearly unseated her, sending her careening to the water. She heard Salazar shout in dismay as Gwendolyn used the rudder to right their boat and she settled herself back in, her hands griping the rail of the small boat so hard, the knuckles of her hands turned white.

"Are you alright?" Gwendolyn called to her.

"Yes," Audrina called back, trying not to sound as if she'd just been terrified. She resumed her post, looking for any sign that their journey was at an end. She was cold now. The lack of sunlight lent a chill to the air. She shivered and her hands started to cramp from gripping the deck so tightly. She couldn't wait for this to be over. She longed to feel the solidity of the ground under her feet again. Ground that wouldn't rock with the waves. Ground that stayed in one place and gave her a sense of stability. Ground that was poking its glorious head out of the waves a short distance away. "Land!" Audrina shouted. "Land is straight ahead! We found it!"

Gwendolyn let out a laugh of relief and happiness. Salazar called out his own happiness that they could soon make anchor. Taking it slow and careful, they steered the boat in the direction of the island ahead, and hopefully towards those they'd lost.

* * *

Lucas and Zayna sat, arms around one another on the beach. He was feeling content being in her company, a feeling that not too long before he hadn't thought was possible. He smiled as he watched the sea. They had spent the day enjoying one another's company, wandering the beach, going into town, talking and laughing with one another. Now, as the sun was setting, they sat and watched, enjoying the view.

"Do you think Finn will find her?" Lucas asked.

"He's the chief," Zayna replied. "He was selected because he knows this island, he knows the people, and he knows when to ask for help. If anyone can figure this out, I believe that he can."

"Zayna, I have to thank you." Lucas pulled her closer so that he was supporting her weight with his body.

"For what?"

"For being you, and for accepting me. You have made me really happy, something that I never thought was possible. I love you, Zayna."

"I love you, too." Zayna turned and drank in the sight of Lucas' smile. The setting sun burnished his dark brown hair a shining copper. She stared at him, as if memorizing the planes of his face. Suddenly she was struck by the sick feeling that this couldn't last. She shook her head, thinking she was being ridiculous. It was just the stress of everything that had happened making her paranoid. Everything would be fine. She'd found love. She'd found happiness, and once they found Gertrude, everything would be perfect.

Lucas looked away from Zayna for a moment, watching the sky. He frowned, narrowing his eyes at a tiny bobbing shape. He tried to make it out, and his frown deepened. He knew that shape, and it spelled trouble.

Zayna felt Lucas stiffen behind her. She followed his gaze and her breath caught in her throat. She should have known. Nothing good stays. Everything ends. She could feel it. "A boat," she breathed.

"What does this mean?" Lucas asked. "What do we do?"

"We go tell Finn." Zayna stood and brushed the sand from her legs. "Come. He needs to know about this."

Lucas nodded and ran off in Zayna's wake, following her to the council building. His earlier happiness and sense of calm had been replaced with dread.

The two of them tore through the streets, barely registering the looks of surprise and the curses hurled their way as they dodged carts, stands, pedestrians and guards en route to the council building. Lucas felt as if his life depended on Finn being told what they'd seen, and he knew that Zayna's panic-stricken face was largely his fault. He breathed heavily through the stitch in his side, each breath a stab in the lungs. Somehow he knew. He knew that the boat they'd seen was not an innocent merchant vessel. It was too small for that. He also knew that it wasn't some couple off on a pleasure cruise. He knew that the people on that boat were there for him and for Gertrude. He couldn't let them take him away. Not when he'd finally found his place.

Zayna barrelled through the doors to the council building and doubled over gasping for breath. Lucas practically careened right into her, sweat dripping down his face. "Where do we go?" he wheezed.

Zayna jerked her head in the direction of the main hall and started trotting down it, all the while, looking for some sign that Finn was nearby. She saw the odd glances she was getting from everyone they passed. Both she and Lucas were hot, sweaty messes, sand still clinging to their feet and clothes from their time on the beach. In contrast, everyone else was well put together, clean and polished for their time working indoors. Occasionally, Zayna would see one of the other councillors and she would pause in her search and politely inquire after Finn's whereabouts. Each time, they would plead ignorance, but promise to tell him that she was looking. Lucas didn't see the point. He viewed each of them through a veil of distrust.

Turning a corner, Lucas saw Jerusha walk smoothly towards them as if she hadn't a care in the world. His insides constricted, and his sweat ran cold down his back. She saw him and smiled warmly. He felt queasy.

"Lucas," she called out to him and hurried forward. She stopped as he did and looked him over. Seeing him in this state, hair mussed, clothes dirty, face red and soaked with sweat gave her cause for concern. "Is everything alright? What's happened?"

Lucas opened his mouth, but no sound came out. He wasn't sure what he could say. He was convinced that she would see through any lie he could tell.

"We're in a bit of a hurry," Zayna said. "My father sent us. He needs to see Chief Councilman Finn. I'm sorry. I'm not even certain what it's about. But I know that my father has been quite upset over the disappearance of Gertrude. He'd come to care about her, in spite of the short period of time." She smiled sweetly at Jerusha and coyly looked at Lucas. "I'm sure you can understand the sentiment."

"Of course," Jerusha said. "I think we both can understand the sentiment in that. Last I saw Finn, he was in his study. Perhaps you can find him there?"

"Th—thank you," Lucas stammered. He made a show of how winded he was, thinking she might think his awkwardness was due to his exertion, and followed Zayna to Finn's study.

They approached the door together and Zayna reached out and took Lucas' hand and gave it a supportive squeeze. "Everything will work out," she said to him. "Trust me on this."

"I trust you on everything." Lucas stood for a brief moment in the quiet of the evening. Outside a window, Lucas could see a pale sliver of moon. He heard cicadas singing in the trees. He could almost pretend that nothing was happening, that the feeling that his life was about to spiral apart once more was just his imagination. But in an instant, the moment was over, and he raised his hand to knock.

"Come in." Finn's gruff voice was heard from inside, and Lucas and Zayna pushed the door open and walked in. Finn looked up to see them and he offered them a grim smile.

"Chief," Zayna said with a brief bow.

Lucas nodded to him and received a nod back. Finn's eyes narrowed as he took in the state of them. He chose to ignore it, focusing on what he felt was pressing.

"I found the entrance to the cells," Finn said. "I have sent someone to go and fetch your father. If Gertrude has been down there, we will probably need him to help her."

Lucas gave a jerky nod of his head. Thinking of Gertrude alone and trapped in the dark made him feel awful. Of all the people he knew, she probably deserved it the least. "Thank you, Chief Councilman."

"Of course." Finn reached out and squeezed Lucas' shoulder. "Once Marcus arrives, we can go and fetch her."

"You really believe she's down there?" Lucas asked.

Finn raked his hands through his hair. Lucas couldn't help but smile. He had seen his father perform that very gesture on numerous occasions. With King Navor, it usually meant that he was frustrated or stymied in his plans. He felt that it probably meant something similar with Finn.

"Honestly, I can't see where else she could be." Finn sighed. "I have eyes everywhere else on this island. The other option, and I am sorry for having to say this, is that she is dead."

Lucas drew in a short breath. Dead. Gertrude could not be dead. He refused to believe that.

"Keep faith, Lucas," Finn assured him. "We still have hope. We will descend to the cells shortly."

"Thank you," Zayna said. "However, we came here with other news. Although, if you have eyes everywhere, you may already know."

"Know what?" Finn felt uneasy. No one had interrupted his work. No one had dared. He had made it clear that he was not to be disturbed.

"Lucas and I were on the beach together, and we saw a boat. It looked as if it was headed straight for Coralnoss. I thought you should be the one to decide what to do about it. We came directly to you, so that you could handle it and decide how it should be dealt with."

"Thank you." He frowned. "Who do you think these people are? Did you see any defining features of the craft?"

"The boat was too far away for us to make anything out," Lucas said. "We ran all the way here."

Finn groaned. He hated when he felt he was being pulled in two. "Unfortunately, we need to push dealing with the dark cells to later. These trespassers need to be dealt with, as I don't believe they will turn around and not come ashore."

Lucas wanted to shout his frustrations. Like Finn, he felt he was being torn in two. He wanted to run down to the cells and see that Gertrude was there and free her. At the same time, he couldn't shake the sinking feeling of dread that the boat making its way to Coralnoss' shores was there for him.

"Come with me," Finn demanded as he grabbed a cloak and walked out of his office. Along the way, he called over a couple guardsmen. "Accompany me to the beach. We may be having some unexpected guests on our shores."

Zayna saw the guardsmen's unease at this news. She too was feeling it. "You need us to come with you?" she asked Finn.

"I do," Finn said. His expression softened as he saw the nervous looks on Lucas and Zayna's face. "You saw the boat. You need to show us where. Lucas, you're not saying anything about this, but I was not voted the chief of the council because I don't see what's in front of me. You're scared of this boat."

"I am," Lucas admitted. As they spoke, he was painfully aware that they were still being propelled through the hall and back out the building. "What if they're here looking for me?"

"Then we will deal with that if and when it comes up." Finn clapped Lucas on the back. "You should know by now that I endeavour to be fair."

Lucas nodded, although he was cognizant of the fact that Finn had not said he would keep him on the island. But he chose to give him the benefit of the doubt. He and Zayna led the way back to the beach. Back to their spot where they had watched the boat approaching. Now it was close enough to see the colours of the sails, and Lucas' heart dropped as he recognized the colours of his grandfather's kingdom. He reached out and pulled Zayna close, trying to get some comfort from knowing that she stood by his side. Behind him, he could hear Finn barking orders to his men, sending one back to the building to convene an emergency council meeting. They would need one to decide what to do with these newcomers. Lucas knew that his secrets would soon be out to the entire council, and the island as a whole.

The small boat kept coming. In the pale moonlight, Lucas saw a flash of blue, and his heart skipped a beat. Surely it wasn't his mother coming all this way for him? But he knew that this was highly unlikely. As it was, he knew that she had neglected the kingdom for far too long. This left his sister. Audrina had come for him and Gertrude. He felt a lump form in his throat at the thought of telling his sister that Gertrude had vanished and was likely locked away from all light and human contact. No. He would tell her that they were on the verge of rescuing her. They would get her back.

"Do you know these people?" Finn asked. He was watching Lucas' face seeing the fear, followed by wistfulness, followed by nerves.

"I…I think so," Lucas said. "The colour of the sail indicates that this boat is one that belongs to my grandfather."

Finn nodded, aware that Lucas had left out who this grandfather was. "What can you tell me about who is on this boat?"

"They're still too far away to make out, but the colour of the hair of one of them…I think that it may be my sister."

Finn nodded. He turned to the guardsmen that flanked them on either side. "Weapons down. I think we should look as if we are friendly. I don't think we should anticipate a fight. But be prepared for anything."

Lucas watched as the guards took a position of feigned relaxation. He tried to level out his breathing and stay calm. He could conjure up a wind and blow the boat back out to sea. For a hysterical moment, he considered doing just that. But he didn't want to risk hurting those onboard. If this was Audrina, she could take Gertrude home with her. That would be best for all. All he had to do was convince everyone of that.

The boat came close to shore, and Zayna watched as an anchor was dropped. Three people clambered out and waded through the waves onto the sand. In the moonlight, she saw two women accompanied by a tall man with long black hair. She glanced over and saw the conflicting emotions flickering over Lucas' face. "It will all work out," she whispered to him. He favoured her with a small smile. She saw the strangers approach, and her eyes widened as she took in the long blue hair crowning the head of one of the women. The blue-haired woman scanned the beach, and upon seeing Lucas, she let out an ecstatic gasp and ran over, pulling him into a tight embrace.

Chapter Twenty-One
Reunions

Audrina couldn't stop the restless hum of energy that coursed through her body. She did what she could to help anchor the boat just off shore of the island. From where they were, she could just make out the tops of buildings poking up over the dunes, and in the moonlight, she could see a small group of people watching them from the beach. She hoped that, whoever they were, they could lead her to her brother, and to Gertrude. That would be a lucky break. But, with her luck, they would probably just tell her that the people she searched for weren't even on the island and they should move on and search elsewhere.

Salazar declared their boat secure, and he jumped down into the shallow water. Gwendolyn followed with Audrina right behind her. They waded through the waves, and as they got closer, Audrina saw one of the people on the beach stiffen. She squinted, almost too scared to believe it, but she knew that head of curly hair, that restless energy, that figure. She let out a cry of joy and surged forward until she was holding her brother tightly in her arms.

"Lucas! You have no idea how long we've been searching. We've been so scared. Are you alright? What happened? Why couldn't you talk to us? We love you so much! Mother and Father were devastated. They miss you terribly. *I* missed you terribly!" Audrina couldn't stop the flow of words, or the flow of tears as she hugged Lucas tightly to her. "I love you so much, you idiot! You should know that by now! I thought you did!"

Lucas let go of Zayna, and before he knew it, he was hugging his sister back. He heard every word she said, and it fuelled his guilt. Of course he knew that what he had done would hurt her and his parents. But didn't she realize how necessary it had been? At the same time, he knew now that this was a hollow rationalization. With the peace he had found on Coralnoss, he viewed all that had happened in a slightly different light. He saw how he had hurt his family, but at the same time, he knew he could not give up the new life he had crafted. He couldn't just leave Zayna behind and be a prince once more.

Gwendolyn watched the reunion with bated breath. If Lucas was here, then that meant… She scanned the beach quickly and her stomach dropped as she realized that Gertrude was not with them. She quickly tried to write off her worry by telling herself that her daughter was probably in a village somewhere, or just hadn't accompanied them. But that seemed unlikely. If a boat had been spotted, and this party of people was there with Lucas, why wouldn't her daughter have come? It seemed as if they were expected. She waited for Audrina to pull away from Lucas before clearing her throat.

"Gwendolyn," Lucas said, and he stepped forward and hugged her.

"Lucas, where is Gertrude?" Gwendolyn asked. "Is my daughter here?"

Lucas pulled away, looking uncomfortable. "It's complicated."

"Uncomplicate it then," she said.

Finn had been watching the entire exchange from a short way back, flanked by his guards. He stepped forward, sensing the woman's distress. "I believe that some introductions are in order, Lucas," he said. "I am Finn, the chief of the council of Coralnoss, and you are on our land."

"Chief," Lucas said with a shallow bow. "This is my sister, Audrina of Colonodona, and our dear friend Gwendolyn. She is Gertrude's mother." He turned and saw Salazar standing behind Audrina. "And this is…"

"I am Salazar," Salazar said with a smile. He copied Lucas' bow, seeing that Finn was a man who demanded respect on this island. "I am a friend to the family."

"You don't know this one?" Finn said to Lucas.

"He doesn't," Audrina answered. "Salazar was a guest of our grandparents. We became friends, and as a skilled sailor, he offered to help me find my brother and Gertrude. If we are intruding on your land, I apologize. We mean no harm or disrespect."

Finn nodded, accepting her apology and feeling happy about the differential treatment he was receiving from her.

Gwendolyn watched the exchange, her anxiety mounting. They mentioned Gertrude's name a few times, so she had to be here somewhere. But where? "My daughter," she burst out. "Where is she? Can I see her?"

Lucas flinched as if she'd slapped him, and the reaction stopped her cold. She looked to see if Audrina had noticed and saw the princess had gone pale.

"Lucas?" Audrina asked. She reached out and touched his arm. "Lucas, where is Gertrude?"

"What happened to my daughter?" Gwendolyn felt the world spin underneath her feet. *Please let her be alright,* she thought. *Please let everything be okay.*

"We don't really know," Lucas admitted. "We have some ideas as to where she is. It's a long story."

"Start telling it," Gwendolyn grit out.

"In due time," Finn said. "We need to take you to the council building. We do not normally accommodate outsiders, and I need to take you to speak with the rest of the council. They will help me ascertain your truthfulness. Then I will tell you what I know."

"With all due respect, we will not be doing that," Gwendolyn said angrily. She saw Lucas give her a warning look, and felt Audrina grip her arm to stop her from lunging at Finn. "I'm sorry, if you think me rude right now. Actually, no. I'm not. I am a mother whose daughter has been missing for quite some time. I am this close to finding her, or at least finding out what happened to her." She paused as she tried to calm herself. She refused to think of her daughter being hurt, or worse. It was too much to bear. "You know something, and you will tell me now. I don't know if you have kids, but if you did, you would never try to keep a parent from theirs. Not for a council meeting, not for anything. Do you understand? I want my daughter!"

Finn listened to her and he knew that she would not come quietly. To bring her before the council like this would not do. "Alright," he said. "My apologies. But, perhaps if we walk while we speak?"

Gwendolyn nodded. She knew she was being handled by him, but if she got her answers, she would allow it. Finn took her, Audrina, and Salazar in stride and told them everything that had happened. Lucas followed close behind with Zayna, half listening to what the chief was saying, and half focusing on the turmoil in his head.

Zayna watched him carefully as they walked. She tried to smile at him. "Your sister seems nice," she said.

"Yes."

"And Gertrude's mother?"

"Also nice."

"You didn't introduce me."

"I—" Lucas fumbled for a reply. "I'm sorry."

"It's okay," Zayna said. "Things seem a bit overwhelming right now. There will be time later."

"I know." Lucas sighed. "I don't know what's going to happen. I don't like it."

"What's going to happen is that we will find Gertrude, meet the council with your sister, have a visit, and then she will go home with Gertrude." Zayna felt that if she said it out loud, then surely that's how it would all work out.

"Do you promise?" Lucas was not so sure.

"I love you, and you love me," Zayna said. "How else could it work out?"

Lucas nodded. He would hold on to her optimism. Maybe it would rub off on him. He jumped back as Audrina turned and ran back to join him. She seemed angry and frustrated. "Is this all true?" she asked. "Gertrude is missing because of your teacher?"

"It's a little more complicated than that," Lucas said, sounding defensive. "It's because my teacher was afraid of exposing what I am." He kept his voice low, trying to ensure no one heard.

"A wizard?" Audrina was confused. Why would anyone care that her brother was a wizard? Especially if he was learning magic.

"No!" Lucas said. He saw Zayna fidget beside him. "By the way, Audrina, this is Zayna. She is the healer's daughter and I love her."

"I'm sorry we had to meet in these circumstances," Zayna said.

"Oh!" Audrina took in the kind expression in Zayna's eyes, and she blushed. "I'm sorry we were so rude."

"It's understandable," Zayna said. "What you need to understand about our island is that we are not a monarchy. We were once, a long time ago. But our rulers were cruel and enslaved the people. They were overthrown and exiled. Since those days, we have been led by our council. This changes with each election. We choose our own rulers from the best and wisest of us."

"So, when you say that your teacher was afraid to expose what you were…" Audrina caught on to what was being unsaid. "Gertrude had what? Wouldn't she have known?"

"It was in a letter," Lucas said. "She had written a letter home to let everyone know we were alive. She didn't want to leave everyone fearful that we may have died. The letter was given to my teacher to give to the council to send it off the island."

"She must have mentioned what you were in it. Who our parents are." Audrina saw exactly what had happened. "Is your teacher a cruel woman?"

"Never to me," Lucas said. "But I have learned rumours and gossip about her. As we both know, there are many sides to a person."

"Indeed." Audrina's expression darkened, as she thought of Lettie, and of King Parven's last conversation with her.

"Audrina," Zayna said. "I know about your connection with Gertrude. My father and I both worked very closely with her since she arrived here. She is strong. We will find her."

"Thank you," Audrina said with a soft smile.

They approached the council building as a group and Gwendolyn paused in the doorway. "Now, take me to my daughter." She stood firm waiting for Finn to do just that.

"We need to meet with the council," Finn said. "It would be preferable to do so with you as willing guests as opposed to people I have apprehended on the beach."

Lucas saw the situation unravelling and he stepped forward with an idea forming in his mind. "Chief," he said. "If I may, might it not be better if we fetch Gertrude first? I assume that you haven't informed the council about all that my teacher has done." He gave a nervous glance to the guardsmen, but they stood feigning disinterest. "If we get Gertrude, then we can deal with both issues at once. Her mother has come for her, and you can expose certain people for what they've done."

Finn thought Lucas' suggestion over. "You are a bright boy, Lucas. Don't think I don't know that your motivation is more about finding your friend."

Lucas smiled sheepishly. "That and I don't wish the council to meet my family as hostile prisoners."

"Alright. We'll go find Gertrude." He turned back to the guardsmen and instructed them to fetch torches. "Come back and meet me in front of my study." They nodded and marched off. Finn led them into the building where they found Marcus waiting.

"Chief," Marcus said. "I came because I heard that we were going to—" he stopped as Finn held up a hand to silence him.

"Audrina, Gwendolyn, Salazar, this is Marcus. He is a healer on this island, and I trust him."

Marcus surveyed the group of people, and he smiled as he saw Audrina. "You must be Lucas' sister."

"And you must be Zayna's father," Audrina said. "I wish we were meeting under better circumstance. Gwendolyn is Gertrude's mother."

"Your daughter is a wonderful girl," he said to her. "She told me everything that you taught her. She's learned well."

"Thank you," Gwendolyn replied. Her eyes looked misty and she was filled with pride. Now all she needed to do was find her daughter.

Finn declared the conversation over and led everyone through the main foyer and around the spiralling corridor. They came up to the door of Finn's study to find the guards there, lit torches at the ready. Finn held out a hand and one of the guardsmen walked to his side and handed him his torch. "Kindly tell the council that an emergency came up and we will be with them as soon as we can."

"Yes, sir." The guard turned and trotted off back in the direction they had just come.

"Where do we go from here?" Zayna asked.

"Just follow me," Finn said and walked off down a small corridor that shot off from the main hall. He walked and followed one hallway, then another until they came to a door that led out to a small garden in the back of the building. He looked around to ensure that no one but them was within view and led them to a large boulder engraved with some odd spiralled markings. He remembered all he'd read about the monarchs and how they'd built their dark cells and pressed the largest mark. He waited a moment, unsure if he'd done it correctly, but was rewarded with a low scraping sound as the boulder moved aside, exposing a large black staircase. Finn leaned over and looked down, allowing the flame to shine down. He turned back and gave them a grim smile. He allowed the guard that remained to lead the way down into the inky darkness to go and find Gertrude.

Chapter Twenty-Two
Descent

Zayna walked slowly down the stairs. The footsteps echoed all around them, the slapping of bare feet intermingling with the clopping of heeled boots on stone. The flames from the torches wavered and flickered against the walls of the long, winding stairwell and she could barely see a few feet ahead. Behind her, Lucas kept close. In front of her, her father walked closely with the newcomers, who, in turn, kept close to Finn and the guard who led the way. Zayna was certain that they would find Gertrude somewhere below, but she couldn't shake the feeling of trepidation that had settled inside of her.

The descent into the dark cells seemed to go on forever. She didn't know how far down they had travelled, but she felt as if they had climbed down a mountain of stairs. In time, her eyes adjusted to the darkness and the firelight from the torches. She could see that the walls on either side was the same rough-hewn black stone of the stairs, and it was all slick and dripping with moisture. They reached the bottom and Finn led the charge. Zayna saw windowless doors flanking them on either side, and Finn went from door to door testing them to see if they opened. So far, none of them were locked or barred, and each cell was empty.

"Gertrude?" Lucas called. "Gertrude! We're here! We've come to get you out of here!"

Audrina turned to Zayna. In the torchlight, Zayna could see the princess' face drawn and pale. "Did you know of this place?" she asked.

"No one did," Zayna said.

"No. Lucas' teacher did. She knew, and she stuck Gertrude down here." Audrina took a deep, shuddering breath. "I can't imagine my Gertrude being trapped in a place like this. It's something out of a nightmare down here." Audrina shivered. The very air felt cold and damp. This was the type of place where hope went to die.

"We'll find her," Zayna assured Audrina. "Have faith."

Audrina nodded. She joined Lucas in calling Gertrude's name, clinging to the sliver of hope she had that they would hear a response.

All of a sudden, the group was brought up short. A torch was seen up ahead, and it was coming closer. Someone else was down here, and they were approaching. Finn held up a hand and stepped forward.

"Who's down here?" Finn called.

"Chief Finn?" came a voice in response. "I am Eden, one of your guardsmen. I was assigned down here."

Finn waited until Eden came closer. He nodded to him. "Eden, who assigned you?"

"Councilwoman Jerusha," Eden answered. "She said that the council had ordered a prisoner down here. I and a couple others have been put on rotation, caring for her and ensuring she is fed and secure."

Finn growled under his breath. "Tell me, Eden, where is she? Because I assure you that these were not *my* orders, nor are they the orders of the council as a whole."

Eden visibly blanched at this news. "Follow me," he said and took them to the end of the hall. Audrina and Gwendolyn both rushed forward as Eden pulled out an old, rusty key ring. He inserted a key into the lock, and with a grinding squeal, he unlocked the door. Handing his torch to Salazar, Eden used both hands and pulled heavily on the door to force it open.

"She's inside," Eden said. "I am so sorry, Chief, I had no idea. I thought…"

"I understand," Finn said. "We will talk shortly. Marcus, Gwendolyn, we may need you both."

Marcus and Gwendolyn ran into the cell with Finn who swung the torch around, peering into the blackness of the cell. Audrina stepped forward and peered inside. At first, they saw nothing, but then, a scuffling sound caught their attention and they turned to see her. Gertrude lay huddled in a corner, barefoot, her clothing torn and stained. She whimpered and flinched against the torchlight.

"Gertrude?" Gwendolyn said in a choked voice. It broke her heart to see her daughter in this state. She crept forward and knelt at Gertrude's side. "Sweetheart? It's me. It's your mother."

Gertrude heard the voice. She felt soft fingers stroking her cheek, petting her hair. But she knew it was impossible. Her mother was with King Parven in his castle far away. She may have even gone home at this point. This wasn't real. Curse this place for these dreams! It was beyond cruelty.

Gwendolyn swallowed a sob as she felt her daughter try to bat her hands away from her. "Gertrude, I'm here. I'm here."

"No," Gertrude moaned. Her voice came out weak and hoarse. "You're not real. You can't be real."

"We're real," Lucas said from his place in the doorway. Inside, he cursed Jerusha for what she had done.

Audrina knelt at Gwendolyn's side, and took her hand. "Gertrude, open your eyes. Look at us. We're real. We came to find you. It's going to be okay. We're okay."

Gertrude was terrified to open her eyes. Audrina too? Also impossible. She had heard Lucas calling from the door. *He could find you*, a little voice whispered in her mind. *He could be real. Open your eyes and see.* She screwed her eyes shut tighter. *No. No one will find me*, she argued with herself. *Then prove it. Open your eyes.* Gertrude opened her eyes a sliver. The first thing she registered was that there was light. For the first time in days, she saw light. Here, in her cell, someone had brought torches. Then, she looked further and saw who was holding her hand, who was stroking her hair. Her mother and Audrina were kneeling at her side, comforting her, touching her.

"Gertrude?" Audrina said as she saw Gertrude's eyes open.

"You're real?" Gertrude asked. "You're really here?"

"We are," Gwendolyn said. She helped her daughter sit up and held her tight. "We're here, and we're getting you out of here."

"I want to go home," Gertrude whispered into her mother's ear.

"You will, darling. We'll take you home." Gwendolyn smiled into her daughter's hair. Everything would be alright now.

Gertrude nodded, her head firmly ensconced in the hollow of her mother's neck. Her hand was still being held tightly by Audrina. She sat there, breathing in her mother's scent. She could almost believe that everything would work out. She slowly pulled herself away and turned to see Audrina smiling at her. Audrina reached out and placed her hand on Gertrude's cheek and leaned in and gently kissed her.

"I love you," Audrina said softly. "I love you so much, and I was so afraid I'd never find you."

"I love you, too," Gertrude replied.

"Let's get you out of here," Audrina said.

Gertrude nodded and Gwendolyn and Audrina helped her to her feet. She felt faint and swayed unsteadily. Marcus stepped forward, seeing Gertrude's physical weakness. He looked into her eyes and took in the state of her.

"Finn," he said. "Let's get her out of here. She needs real food, drink, to bathe, and to put on something clean and warm."

"Alright," Finn said. "Let's go. I'm sure we don't want to stay down here longer than we have to."

Finn directed the guards to lead the way back down the corridor towards the stairs. Lucas walked behind them, hearing snatches of their conversation.

"I take it that Gertrude is not the only one the councilwoman has put down here," Finn said.

"I, personally, have not seen others," Eden said.

"I'm inferring from your comment that you do know something," Finn said, shrewdly eyeing the guard at his side.

"Merely rumours and gossip from the other guards." Eden shifted uncomfortably under the chief's stare.

Lucas looked from one man to another, keenly aware that this conversation was not necessarily what he was supposed to be listening to. He listened, thinking back to Finn's words about how all rumours had some bit of truth to them.

"Tell me," Finn coaxed.

"Some of the men have been speaking about duty down here," Eden said. "Every so often, someone is placed in charge of a rotation in these cells. They say that the prisoners weep and they languish here."

"And what becomes of them?" Finn sharply asked.

"They die."

Finn's frown deepened. "I have never sent anyone down to these cells. This is not our way. We are not cruel people."

"I understand," Eden said. "I see now that I was used. My duty down here was unpleasant, to say the least. I was never told who our prisoner was. I was not the one to bring her down here. I am so sorry."

"I see. But your apology needs to be given to Gertrude," Finn said.

"I will give it when she is able to hear it," Eden assured Finn.

"Good."

They reached the stairs and Lucas looked back to see Gertrude swaying unsteadily as she looked up at how far she had to climb. He approached and laid a gentle hand on her shoulder. "May I help?" he asked.

Gertrude mutely nodded.

Lucas murmured a spell and Gertrude felt lighter. She realized that his magic was holding her up and making it easier for everyone to help her up the stairs. She gave him a small smile of thanks.

The group made their way slowly up the stairs and back up into the garden in the back of the council building. Gertrude looked startled when she saw where they were.

"Are you okay?" Zayna asked, seeing the look on her face.

"All this time," Gertrude said in a small voice. "All this time I was right here, and no one knew."

"We still found you," Zayna said. "I'm just sorry it took so long."

"I was still found," Gertrude said. "And look at who came." She smiled at her mother and Audrina. She felt as if she were back where she belonged. She saw Salazar walking past. "I don't know who that is, though."

"I'll explain later," Audrina said with a fond smile. "Now let's do what Marcus said and get you fed and cleaned up."

Feeling exponentially lighter, Gertrude let herself get led inside with the promise of a warm meal and a hot bath.

Chapter Twenty-Three
The Council Meeting

Gertrude emerged from her room a little while later feeling clean and fed, wearing some fresh clothes, her hair brushed and braided. Though she was tired, she knew that there was no way she would miss the council meeting. She had left everyone out in the hall, only taking her mother inside with her to help her if needed. They had spoken while Gertrude had bathed and eaten, and Gertrude had been gratified and relieved to hear that Audrina had told her grandparents all about their relationship, and that her princess had no intention of giving in to her grandparents' desire that she marry some high-born nobleman.

Gertrude now walked into the main corridor outside of her room and approached Salazar with a small smile. "I understand that you're the reason Audrina and my mother are here," she said to him.

Salazar's face flushed at her words. "I don't know if I would put it like that," he said. "They never stopped looking for you. They never lost hope."

"But it was your knowledge and skill that brought them here. Was it not?"

"I…"

"I'm trying to thank you," Gertrude said.

"You are very welcome," Salazar replied.

"If we are now ready," Finn broke in. "We need to get to the council room. I cannot keep them much longer."

The group walked together down the hall and stopped just outside the door to the council room. Gertrude felt as if she were a bundle of nerves. She had been uncomfortable the first time the council had spoken to her. And though it seemed as if Finn was on their side, she still felt distrustful of his allegiance to them. Furthermore, Jerusha was in there. After what had happened in her study; how Jerusha had drugged her and left her to rot in that cell, Gertrude had no desire to see her again, let alone confront her. But she swallowed her trepidation and followed in Finn's footsteps as he opened the door and walked inside.

The rest of the council was already seated and waiting. Finn saw their frustration at the hour and at how long he had kept them waiting. He had to take control now and assert his role as their leader. "Good evening, I apologize for the delay. I assure you that there was a pressing issue to deal with that could not be ignored. You know I would not have delayed you otherwise."

"Finn," Jerusha said. "You know that we are all busy. Wasting our time on frivoliti—" She broke off, and Finn was gratified to hear a sharp intake of breath as her eyes fell onto Gertrude standing just behind him, her hand firmly ensconced in the hand of a young woman with cascading blue hair. She tried to smooth this over with a silky smooth smile. "I see you have found our missing Gertrude, and some more strangers. Finn, what is the meaning of these people? Why are they here? Where did they come from?"

"Jerusha," Finn replied, just as smoothly. "Careful, one would think that you were trying to lead this council meeting. I assure you that *all* of these things will be answered, as this is why I've convened you all tonight."

Jerusha's eyes narrowed as she heard the veiled threat in his words. She could feel that her plans were slowly unraveling. She would not be undone. Not by Finn, not by the others on the council, and certainly not by Gertrude.

The council began muttering among themselves as they sensed the tension between their chief and Jerusha.

"We will all be held accountable by the truth stone as usual," Finn said. He turned to Gwendolyn, Audrina, and Salazar. "The truth stone is the large stone in the centre there," he indicated it for their benefit. "If anyone lies, it will glow red. We will all know."

Audrina regarded it with interest. Such a thing would be beneficial in a trial back at home. She wondered how it worked.

Finn walked over to the council table and took his customary seat in the centre. "People of the council. These newcomers landed on the beach this evening. I was alerted to their presence by Lucas and Zayna who spotted their boat approach, and I went with some guardsmen to greet them. They do not mean us harm, and have come for Lucas and Gertrude, as they are their family."

The councilwoman to Finn's right spoke up at his words. "And what do Lucas and Gertrude wish? They have both proven themselves loyal and useful members of Coralnoss' society."

"Councilwoman Helena, we have offered them safe harbour, and a place to live here. If they wish to stay, I see no issue with it," Finn said.

Lucas' heart soared. He could stay. "I would like to remain here," he said. He put his arm around Zayna's waist and she held him back. "I have created a life here, found love, friendship, everything I've wanted. I wish to stay."

Audrina felt her heart break at hearing her brother's words. But at the same time, she saw how he had found a purpose. He seemed taller, older, wiser here. She knew that her mother and father back home would be saddened at his decision, but she hoped they would come to understand. At least he was alive, and happy.

"And you, Gertrude?" Finn asked.

"I wish to go home with my family," she said in a quiet voice. "It's not that I don't appreciate all you have done for me. I have truly enjoyed meeting you, and working with Marcus and Zayna. They have been nothing but kind and good to me. I don't want to sound ungrateful, but I miss my home too much. And…" she trailed away seeing Jerusha's angry glare in her direction. In it, she saw a warning, a warning to keep her mouth shut.

"My child," Helena said. "Where were you all this time? We had heard you were missing. We had heard that there were people on this island searching for you. People like Marcus, Zayna, and Lucas. What happened?"

"What does it matter?" Jerusha asked sharply. She felt a rising panic within her. It was a feeling she was not too familiar with and she hated it. Usually she had control, and she felt it slipping from her grasp. "What matters is these newcomers. We do not allow people to flit in and out of our land like this. Do you want to go back to the way of kings? We were slaves then. I will not be one now and inviting people who do not understand our ways invites invaders and conquerors." She was gratified by murmurs of agreement all around her.

"Ah, but it matters greatly," Finn said. "We all recognize that this council acts best as a collective. A collective of people who were chosen to cooperate with one another. And when one of us goes rogue, taking matters into his or her own hands…that collective falls apart."

"What are you saying?" said a wizened old man further down the table. "Speak plainly, Finn. Who are you accusing and why?"

"Councilman Hermann, I think we should hear it from Gertrude," Finn genially replied. He gave her an encouraging look and was gratified when she held her head higher and stepped forward.

Inside, Gertrude was shaking. She was terrified. But she refused to let Jerusha see how much she was scared of her. "I never made it a secret that I was homesick, that I missed my mother and father, and that I missed the woman I love. It was suggested that I write a letter home. At least that way I could tell everyone that Lucas and I were unharmed, alive, and well. I wanted at least that for my parents. Losing a child is the worst thing that could happen to a parent. At least I could ease their minds. So, I wrote my letter and gave it to Lucas. He offered to give it to Jerusha who, he reasoned, could pass it on to the council and you all could find a way to send it for me.

"Lucas promised me that he had done that. It helped ease my mind somewhat. It wasn't a perfect solution. I still missed home dreadfully, but it helped. And then, I was told that both Lucas and I had been played falsely. Jerusha would never send the letter. I went to confront her about this. I was hurt. I was angry. She corroborated this and said that she hadn't passed it on, and that she would never pass on any communication that was to be sent off the island. I was greatly distressed, and she gave me a drink. She said it was to calm me. Instead, it caused me to faint away in her study. I remember the drink falling from my hand. I remember the sound of the cup shattering on the floor…" She stopped. She felt the daggers from Jerusha's glare as if they were physically stabbing her.

"Continue, Gertrude," Finn coaxed her. "You are safe here."

"I woke up surrounded by darkness." Gertrude trembled at the memory. "I screamed and screamed, but no one ever answered. I saw no light, except for slivers of it as food was passed to me a couple times a day. I was left alone in a black and cold cell. I don't even know for how long. There was no sunlight, no moonlight, no way of telling the time. It was nothing but blackness for me. I feared I should go mad down there.

"Then, just today, I was rescued by Finn, by Lucas, by Marcus. My family came for me, and here I stand. I shudder to think about what would have happened if they didn't."

"Impossible," Hermann wheezed. "We have no such cells. We would never be so cruel."

"The stone didn't glow once during her story," Helena argued with him.

"The cells exist. I was there myself this very evening." Finn looked from one council member to another. "These cells are left from our former monarchs. When we destroyed their castles, what lay beneath remained. The entrance is through the gardens out back. A few of our guardsmen have been down there thinking they were on council business. They were used most foul. And there is one among us who has put them to use. Gertrude was not the first to languish down there in the dark. The others, I regret to say were not so fortunate. I was informed that they perished."

The council erupted into chaos. One after another began to cry out their disgust at this. Jerusha had had enough.

"I will not sit here and be slandered!" she bellowed. "These are lies!"

Lucas' eyes widened as he saw the truth stone glow red. "No!" he called out. "The only liar here is you. See?"

Finn smugly smiled as he too saw it glow at her protestations. He had long known of her desire to take his place at the next vote. Now he could stop it from happening. He would surely get chosen again after this. The rest of the council settled as they too saw what had happened.

"So it is a crime to try and protect someone?" Jerusha said in a hurt tone of voice.

"Who were you protecting?" Helena asked. "Surely not Gertrude!"

Jerusha looked at her former pupil. He had betrayed her. Gertrude had destroyed her. She saw the noose closing around her neck. Let them all go down with her. "I was protecting Lucas," she said.

Lucas felt the first trickle of worry slide up his spine. This would not go well.

"Protect him from what?" Hermann asked her.

"From all of you," Jerusha snarled. She pointed an accusatory finger at Gertrude. "That little idiot thought that her letter would just get sent off by you. No consequences. No problems. However, it was an invitation. At least, that's how I read it. An invitation to conquerers. Kings, queens, and all that accompany them. And now, your leader, Finn, in all his wisdom has allowed them on our shores, into our council chambers."

"What are you talking about?" Helena said. Her eyes were wide with shock. She looked at the stone, hoping it was glowing red, but it wasn't.

Finn sighed. Jerusha had lobbed a bomb into the proceedings. Sacrifices needed to be made. "She means that Lucas is a prince. He is the prince of a kingdom called Colonodona. That young woman there, with the blue hair," he pointed at Audrina. "She is next in line to the throne, and she is his sister."

He listened to the resulting explosion and felt a stab of hatred as he saw the smug look of satisfaction on Jerusha's face.

"We cannot allow this!" cried another council member. "We have fought so long to keep these people away from our shores!"

Zayna watched and listened to all of this as if she were in a nightmare.

Zayna understood the council's fear. It was a fear that had been drilled into them since birth, just as it had with every person on the island. But that fear couldn't, *shouldn't* extend to Lucas. She saw the panicked expression on Lucas' face and she grit her teeth. They both knew that the council was fully prepared to lump him in with those who had gone before and their gross misdeeds.

"Stop it!" Zayna cried out. She had had enough. "Lucas is not a conqueror. His sister is not an invader! He came here to leave his title and his old life behind.

Didn't you hear his words before? He wishes to live here and be a part of our society and follow our ways. Let him stay and let everyone else leave here in peace. We're not monsters like the old kings and if we destroy these lives, all that we've built will be for nothing. We will be no better than those people we strive to distance ourselves from. Please. Don't destroy this."

"Zayna," Finn said. He kept his voice soft, his tone understanding. As much as it pained him, he knew what he had to do if he wanted to keep control of his council. "I understand your feelings. I don't deny that Lucas is a good man. I don't doubt his sincerity. You love him. That much is clear, and he loves you. It pains me greatly to even conceive of splitting up those in love."

"Thank you, Chief Finn," Zayna said. She was awash with relief. He understood. She felt a surge of hope. Maybe everything would work out after all.

The rest of the council heard Finn's words and half of them cried out in anger, while the others silently considered them. Jerusha heard this and considered her next move carefully. If she was to walk away from this unscathed, she had to tread lightly.

"I found out about Lucas' pedigree only very recently," Finn said. "This was never something I considered keeping from you all. I was going to speak with him first and note his feelings on the matter. All this I was going to put before you for an open and frank discussion. No. We do not accept the monarchy here on Coralnoss. And we would have to look at this from all angles."

"If I may?" Audrina said, stepping forward.

Finn gestured for her to speak.

"Yes, my brother is a prince, and I am a princess," Audrina said. "But, in Lucas' case, he has always been a wizard first. If you were to truly ask him what he considered himself to be, he would never say that he was a prince. Do I want to lose him? Do I truly wish him to stay here? If I were to answer honestly, I would have to say that I do not. I wish for him to return home with me; to be reunited with our parents. We all miss him terribly, and we have all been so awfully worried about him. It would pain me greatly to say goodbye. We love him."

Lucas looked at his sister. What was she trying to do?

"All that being said," Audrina continued, ignoring Lucas' stare. "I also see that he has found a place where he fits. He has found someone he loves who loves him back. This is not something I would ever take away from him. I know what it feels like to be separated from someone who holds your heart." She turned and smiled at Gertrude. "What kind of sister would I be if I were to do that to my brother? I can't say that I love him and then subject him to that pain. If it is the will of the council, I would gladly tell him to stay. I would leave him here with you to continue to build the life he desires.

"You also speak of monarchs and rulers as conquerors and enslavers. I cannot speak to your history, because I am ignorant to it. I do not doubt how your ancestors suffered under the rule of kings. What I can speak to is my own intentions. I desire peace. I was taught to rule through kindness and compassion. Through justice and through treaties. I have no desire to conquer new lands and to take over those where others live in peace and I do not want to take over what you have built here. You have my word on that. If you tell me to go and to never return, if that is your will and your decree, I will abide by it and respect it. That is your right as the ruling body of this land."

"Thank you for your words," Finn said. "We will take them into account. Now, I need to ask you to leave this hall and wait outside the doors. We will deliberate on these matters. Jerusha, as much as I would like you to join them, you are still a part of this council, and have a voice. But know that we speak of your fate as well. I say this out loud here, so that one of your victims can hear my thoughts on this matter." He pointedly looked at Gertrude. "You have shown a callous disregard for another's well-being, and quite probably more than one person has suffered under your rogue judgement. You have attempted to conceal things from the rest of the council, and you have shown contempt for our way of doing things, and for justice and fairness. Things that we hold dear, after the years they were denied to us. As such, we will be judging you this night, as well as the guests we have welcomed to our shore." Finn turned to the guardsmen still standing with Lucas and the others. "Take them to the main hall. We will summon them back inside when we have reached consensus."

Lucas allowed himself to be led away. He was quaking inside. He knew it could go either way. His fate lay in the hands of others, and he was left to wait.

Chapter Twenty-Four
Judgement

Lucas paced up and down the corridor. He hated waiting. He was never good at being patient with anything. Zayna tried to walk with him, but after a while she gave up and sat with her father. Across from them, Gertrude and Audrina sat together with their arms around each other, also waiting to find out the council's decision.

"So, tell me about Salazar," Gertrude said.

"He led me back to you," Audrina replied with a warm smile. "He's a lovely person. He's one of the 'eligible young noblemen' my grandparents want me to meet. However, like myself, he has no desire to marry anyone his parents choose for him. He has no desire to marry at all."

"It's things like this that make me think a place like this has it right," Gertrude said with a sigh. "I can't imagine anyone here being told who they have to be yoked to for the rest of their lives."

"They really choose their own leaders?" Audrina asked thoughtfully.

"From the wisest of their people," Gertrude answered.

"That went so well with Jerusha," was Audrina's sarcastic reply.

Gertrude gave a mirthless laugh. "But she at least was put to heel by the rest of the council. She's not working and making decisions on her own. It seems as if there are some safeguards in place. Who was there to stop King Supmylo when he was ruling?"

"My mother." Audrina frowned, remembering the story of how her mother stood up to them man she called father, at the expense of the life of her friend Najort. "She paid quite a price for it though."

Gertrude nodded. "I'm not saying one way is better than another. You will make a marvellous ruler one day. But it's interesting to see a different form of rule."

"The people on the council seem far more free than I do right now," Audrina said in a quiet voice.

"They do." Gertrude leaned her head against Audrina's shoulder.

"Gertrude," Audrina said. "I know why you felt you had to leave."

"What do you mean?"

"That dinner, at my grandparents' home. You heard my grandmother talking about my marrying someday." She chewed her lip a moment before she spoke again. "I know that part of your reasoning was to care for Lucas, and I am grateful for that, but part of it was my fault. You should know that while you were missing, I told my grandparents about me. About us."

"Audrina! Is everything okay?" Gertrude stared at her in shock. "But, just so you know, I don't blame you for that dinner at all. I do understand why you said nothing then."

"I know," Audrina said. "But I still felt badly about it. It was not a comfortable situation at all. As for my grandparents… My grandmother was quite good about it. I think part of her thinks I just need to meet the 'right' young man."

"Hence, Salazar," Gertrude said with a wry grin.

"Exactly," Audrina replied. She looked down at her dress and fiddled with its folds as she remembered how her grandfather had ranted and raved at her. She didn't know what Gertrude would think.

"I take it from your silence that King Parven was less kind," Gertrude said softly.

Audrina nodded.

"I am so sorry," Gertrude said. She pulled Audrina close and held her tightly.

"He said I was depraved," Audrina said in a small voice.

Gertrude's heart broke. She held Audrina and let her cry, offering her support by merely being there.

Across the hall, Salazar stood with one of the guards. Everything about this place fascinated him: how they ruled, how they built, the spiral hallways, the former monarchy. It was the mystery he'd longed to crack, and now he was there.

"So," Salazar began. "Is there a library here?"

"There is," said the guard.

"How many books are there?" Salazar asked.

"Hundreds."

How Salazar longed to get his hands on some of those volumes and read up on every aspect of this place! He turned back to the guard. "Do you think *I* could—"

"No."

Audrina had stopped crying. She and Gertrude leaned into one another, each the other's support. Gertrude felt an exhaustion down to her very bones. She let it carry her away and started to doze off.

Across the hall, Gwendolyn sat beside Marcus and watched her daughter with a fond look on her face. "Her father will be so happy we found her. I think it would have killed him if we'd truly lost her for good." Gwendolyn looked away to catch Marcus' eye. "Thank you for all you did for her."

"And yet, she still came to harm," he said. "I am so sorry for that."

"We found her in the end," Gwendolyn said. "It will work out, and we will bring her home."

"You raised a remarkable girl," he said. "You should be proud."

"I am. And you should be as well." She watched as Zayna rested, curled up into her father's side. The girl's turquoise hair seemed to glimmer in the torch light. From what she had seen of the healer's daughter, Gwendolyn understood what it was that had drawn Lucas in.

Marcus smiled fondly at Zayna. "After I lost my wife, Zayna became my whole world. She is my family. I couldn't have wished for a better daughter."

"Nor could I." Gwendolyn watched Gertrude sleep. Grateful and hopeful that everyone she cared about would get the happy ending they deserved.

* * *

Lucas waited with baited breath as the doors to the council room slowly opened to readmit them. It was time for them to hear the council's decision regarding their fate. Lucas walked in, struggling to keep the wobble from his gait. Zayna walked at his side, offering support through her proximity to him. At his other side walked Gertrude, similarly flanked by Audrina and Gwendolyn. He caught her trying to give him an encouraging smile, and he tried to return it, but it felt like more of a grimace. He looked up at the members of the council, trying to find some clue as to their decisions in their expression, but all he saw were sombre faces, and he realized that they always looked that way. The one thing he did note was that Jerusha's seat was flanked by two guards, and she looked pale and drawn. He felt a twinge of sympathy in thinking that things had not gone her way. But this sentiment was quickly squashed when he recalled what she had done to Gertrude.

Finn rose as they all filed into the room once more. "Thank you all for your patience. We do not take these things lightly. The responsibility of the council is a weighty one. After all, all the island looks to us for leadership and guidance. Our first order of business deals with Councilwoman Jerusha. Normally, we would be handling this in a more private way, but since this is justice for you, Gertrude, we thought you should hear what we have decided."

"Thank you, Chief Finn," Gertrude said.

167

Finn nodded his acceptance of her thanks. "For her crimes against you and against this council, in breaking our laws of consensus and acting unilaterally, Jerusha is stripped of her title as a member of this council. She will also be imprisoned for the next five years. After this, she may resume her post as a handler of magic, though she will never again be permitted to run for a council post. This is what we have decided." Finn gestured to the guards at either side of her. They took her by the arms and solemnly led her out of the room through a back door.

Gertrude watched this feeling vindicated for what she had gone through. It felt good to her to see their justice in action.

"As to the other matters," Finn continued. "This was more complicated. We have laws against royalty here on this island. It is never permitted. When our last king and queen were exiled, it was decreed that never again would anyone of royal blood be allowed to set foot on our shores. And yet, here you are. Gertrude, you wish to leave. That is your right. We do not wish to keep good people, such as yourself, here against their will. You may go home with your mother and those she came with. Audrina, Crown Princess of Colonodona. You are not permitted to be here. As a royal, you are banished from our land. This is our law, and we will uphold it."

Audrina curtsied low in front of the council. Inside, her heart sang. Gertrude was coming home with her! She looked up at the council and kept her expression solemn. "I accept your judgement, and I will obey," she said.

"We never wish to see your ships in these waters again," Finn said. "If we do, we may have to take a harsher action. We do not want Coralnoss to be invaded by outsiders. We keep to ourselves. We want nothing to do with the problems of kings."

Lucas listened to this exchange. He felt hopeful that, so far, he had been ignored. Part of him was saddened to think that this would be the last time he would see his sister. Finn's words meant that he would never see his mother and father again. He hoped that they would give him time for a proper goodbye. Perhaps he could write a letter for his sister to take home so he could tell his parents all that had happened.

"Now we come to the hardest part of our decision." Finn took a breath and looked at the small group of people before him. "I have to say that there are some of us who still do not feel good about the consensus that we came to, but our reasoning is sound. Lucas."

Lucas looked directly at Finn at the mention of his name. His heart started hammering in his chest and his mouth went dry. He reached out and found Zayna's hand. With her other hand, she rubbed his arm, steadying him.

"You seem like a fine young man. We welcomed you into our world. We watched you fit in among our people and start a life, find love, and work on your vocation. You are an asset to Coralnoss. However, we also find you a liability." Finn watched as Lucas opened his mouth to argue, and he shook his head. Lucas saw and shut his mouth once more. "As much as everyone says you have renounced your title as a prince, royalty is a blood right. You cannot renounce blood. If your sister ascended the throne and died childless, would Colonodona leave you be here? Or would we once more have conquerors invading our shores? Would they not come for you? We believe they would. Coralnoss is safer cut off from the kingdoms of the other islands and the mainlands. We wish to remain as we were: isolated and safe. As much as it pains us to do this to you, Lucas, you need to go with your family and return to your home."

Lucas could take no more of this. "My home is here!" he said. He felt his eyes fill with tears, and he let them fall. "I fit in here! I belong here!" He looked from Zayna to Marcus, his gaze pleading with them for help.

"Members of the council," Zayna said. "Please reconsider. I love him, and he loves me. We belong together. Please!"

"We do not take pleasure in causing you pain," Helena said. "But in time, these wounds will heal. We cannot put the happiness of one over the safety of so many others."

Marcus looked at his daughter, and at the pain on her face. His heart broke for her, but the laws were there for a reason and could not be broken. Not even for love.

"What if I went with him?" Zayna said.

With her words, it felt as if Marcus' broken heart had just been ripped from his chest. Could he allow his daughter to go?

"Oh, child," Helena sighed. "To think of a child of Coralnoss leaving the sanctuary of our island for the prison of a palace. You would wither and die in those walls. Finn, could we permit that?"

Finn looked at the anguished face of Zayna and turned to look at her father. Marcus, seeing that everyone else was focused on the lovers, he quickly shook his head. *No! Don't take her from me.* He didn't know if Finn understood. If Zayna knew she would hate him for it, but she was all he had. How could he let her go?

"I don't think we could," Finn slowly said. "It is one thing for one such as Gertrude to go. She was born and bred within their ways. You know our secrets. You know who we are, what we come from. I don't like the idea of one of us living among them. It is sacrilege. Are we agreed?"

Zayna watched, blood draining from her face as one by one, the council voted and agreed with Finn and Helena. Only wizened old Hermann disagreed.

"Keep someone away from one they love? Disgraceful! For what? Let her go and be miserable. What do I care?" he wheezed.

169

Zayna felt as if the vote had been a death knell. She and Lucas clung to one another in the centre of that room, knowing that they were to be torn apart.

"Please," she whispered. "Don't do this." But it was too late.

Finn declared the meeting adjourned, and accompanied by guards, Lucas and Gwendolyn were taken to pack their things to go. They were to leave at dawn. Zayna coaxed the guards into letting her stay at his side, and together, they spent the remainder of their night in each other's arms, memorizing each other as best they could, before their final goodbye.

Chapter Twenty-Five
Departure

Zayna lay in Lucas' bed, staring at the planes of his face, drinking in every eyelash, freckle, and curve, forming a detailed picture in her mind. Here was a man who washed up on her beach and had changed her life, and now with the tide, he was going to leave once more. It didn't seem fair. It didn't seem right! Why couldn't everyone see they belonged together? Zayna needed to have some way for him to remember her, and she knew exactly what that was.

"Do you have everything you need?" Zayna asked him.

"No," Lucas said. "How could I? I don't have you."

She smiled sadly at him. "I know, but clothing, your bag. What about those things?"

Lucas sighed. He didn't see the point of packing. None of this stuff fit in Colonodona.

"Let me," Zayna said. She got up and threw some clothes into a small pack for him, then crossed over to the small table in the corner of the room and grabbed one more thing. Lucas watched as she busied herself at the table for a few moments. He didn't see what she was doing, but he drank in her presence for as long as he could. She crossed back to the bed and set the bag down.

"Humour me," she said softly. "Take at least a few things from here. Okay?"

Lucas nodded. "I wish I could stay here," he said. "But I see their point. As much as I hate it. As much as I want them to be wrong. If something were to happen, and I end up the heir, I know the people of my family's kingdom. They would never let me be. And I could never bring that here."

"Now you're thinking like a prince," Zayna said. "But you're also thinking like a leader, and you're putting our safety over your happiness." She sighed. "It seems so stupid to think in these hypotheticals! I wish you didn't have to. I wish we could just live our lives free of these responsibilities and worries."

"So do I," Lucas replied. "It's partly why I ran. My whole life feels lived in hypotheticals. I'm sure my sister's does too: what if she finds some way to be with Gertrude for the rest of her life? What if she never births an heir? What if I become king? Everything feels random and unfair, yet we always have to be prepared for any of these scenarios." Lucas rose and swore as he walked across the room. "Why couldn't I have been born a farmer? Or maybe a fishmonger?" He laughed, but there was very little humour in it.

"You probably would have never met me," Zayna said.

"That would have been awful. As much as this hurts, I will always be grateful for our time together." He sat down beside her once more and kissed her deeply.

"As will I," Zayna said. She sat with her arms around his waist, breathing him in, making one more memory of their time together.

A knock on the door broke them apart. Wide-eyed they both looked out the window to see the sky tinged pink with the approaching dawn.

"Sorry to intrude," called a guard from outside their door. "It's time to go."

Slowly, reluctantly, Lucas and Zayna rose from the bed and opened the door. Zayna was finding it hard to find the words to speak.

"I truly am sorry," the guard repeated.

"I know," Lucas replied.

In the early hours, the council building was nearly empty, save for Lucas, Zayna, Audrina, Gertrude, Gwendolyn, Salazar, Marcus, and their guards. But as they approached the door to leave, they saw Finn step forward to meet him.

"Why?" Zayna asked as she saw him.

"I felt I should say my farewells," Finn replied.

"No. Why did you do this?" she asked.

"I obey the council's consensus," he said. "Fighting them all is fighting a losing battle. I am not magical, and I cannot say some spell to make them agree with me. Even if I could, that would be a gross violation of their trust in me and in my position. Zayna, I am not a monster. I am a leader, and this is what the council feels is best for all of Coralnoss."

"Not all," Zayna said.

Finn watched as the group was ushered outside, then reached out and pulled Zayna back. "And what about your father?" he whispered. "I remember what he was like when your mother died. You kept him afloat. You gave him something to cling to, to live for. Would you abandon that man for someone you've known for such a short time? I know you feel you love Lucas. I believe you when you say you do but think of Marcus. What would it do to him if you run off knowing you could never return?"

"I—" Zayna said. She watched her father walking and talking with Lucas. She barely remembered what it had been like when her mother had died. When she tried to all she remembered was darkness and tears.

"I'm not saying your situation is an easy one," Finn said. "But I am saying is that it does not only affect you. Your decisions affect a great many people around you, and you should consider that before trying to leap onto a boat and sail away."

"I wasn't going to do anything like that!" Zayna protested.

"Of course not," Finn said with a knowing smirk. "But now, we need to go down to the beach."

The day looked as if it were going to be clear and bright. A light breeze blew off the sea, and already, Lucas could see the mermaids frolicking in the surf. It was the opposite to the turmoil he felt inside. He hated it.

"I'm sorry, Lucas," Finn said, stepping forward and taking the prince's hand. "I truly am, and I want you to know that I do wish you well."

"I know," Lucas said. Looking into the chief's eyes, he could almost believe he meant every word. "Know that I mean it when I say thank you. Your island helped me see what was good again. I thought I had lost that. Coralnoss is a special place, and even though I won't be here, a piece of my heart will."

"Safe travels." Finn gave a small bow to Lucas, and Lucas bowed back. "Safe travels to you all," he said to the rest of them.

Gertrude hugged Marcus tightly. "I learned a lot from you here," she said. "Keep doing good work."

"And you as well," Marcus said. "I am so glad we found you."

"Thank you once more for caring for my daughter," Gwendolyn said to him.

"She is a fine girl," Marcus replied. "Safe travels to you both."

Gertrude hugged Zayna goodbye as well and waded through the surf with her mother to where Audrina and Salazar were already on their boat, preparing it for sail.

Lucas watched them a moment, feeling as if he could just run to town and let them go, but he knew that this was a foolish idea.

"I couldn't think of a better match for my daughter," Marcus said, placing a hand on Lucas' shoulder. "I wish this had a happier ending."

"You and me both," Lucas replied. "Look, I…I don't know what to say. You have been so kind to me, and I have nothing to offer in return. I don't want to have to go. I think of you as my family now, just as I do Gwendolyn and Gertrude. I know what the council said, but it shouldn't be all about blood. Some things run far deeper than that."

"You're right," Marcus replied. "And maybe one day, more people will understand that. But until that day comes, you live your life the best you can. Some days are glorious, and others are days like today."

"I wish it wasn't so," Lucas said. "But, thank you. For everything."

"You too, son." Marcus felt himself enveloped in a crushing hug. He felt guilty, as if he'd had a part of this, but he swallowed the feeling down, telling himself this was for the best. It was best for Zayna this way. He broke away. "Safe travels, Lucas."

"Thank you, Marcus." Lucas turned to Zayna who ran at him and kissed him fiercely.

"I love you," she whispered when they broke apart. "I love you and no time or distance will change that."

"I love you, too," Lucas said. "I will not believe this is the end. Keep hope, Zayna."

"Safe travels," Zayna said and pulled away.

Lucas held back his tears and waded to the boat. Salazar helped him up and they cast off. Lucas sat on the edge of the deck watching as Zayna, then the island faded from view. When he could see no more, he still sat and stared. He didn't know how much time passed, he just knew that the sun was high in the sky when Gertrude sat down beside him.

"Audrina is planning the best way to surprise your mother," she said. "She thinks that Sitnalta will scream, then cry. My mother is convinced it will be the other way around."

Lucas had to laugh at that. "They're both wrong."

"Oh?"

"I think she'll faint," he said.

"Want to make a wager on it?" Gertrude asked.

"No," Lucas replied. "Once I do, I will automatically lose."

"Just so you know," Gertrude said. "I accidentally went into your pack thinking it was mine. They look identical. I'm sorry."

"It's alright."

"Well, Salazar saw something and nearly had a fit he was so excited. Apparently, he's a big nautical history scholar, or something." Gertrude giggled. "But I kept it out of his reach. I thought you should take a look." She pressed a book into Lucas' hands and left him alone in his spot.

Lucas turned the book over and his eye widened. It was Jerusha's book on the history of Coralnoss. He flipped through the pages until he came to the illustration of the king and queen going into exile. Their blue hair and haughty expressions gleamed in the sunlight. Lucas stared at them wondering why Zayna had put this into his pack, and then he saw her note, hastily scribbled into the margins:

> *This is not goodbye. This is only until we meet again. I love you, my exiled prince. Never forget where you came from, and never forget where you belong. I will find you. Have hope. Have faith.*

> *— Forever yours,*
> *Zayna*

Epilogue

Zayna stood on the shore and watched the waves. Her eyes tracked the horizon, watching for the small boat that had bobbed on the waves. The painted sails of the vessel had long since disappeared. Mermaids swam in the wake, their multi-hued heads dotting the surf like jewels in the setting sun. One of her hands slowly rose in a futile wave of farewell. She knew he couldn't see it, but her heart hoped he would know that she had gone down to their beach, that she had lingered there; waiting and watching.

The waves lapped at her feet. Her toes sunk in the sand. Her footprints had long faded away. If she turned to look, she wouldn't be able to see the path she had taken to reach that spot. It felt as if everything in her life was as temporary. Things and people came into her life to make a mark and then vanished without a trace. Nothing lasted. But no. She would not follow that train of thought. She thought of the happy times she had had. Her father, Lucas. They were her anchor.

But Lucas had been sent away. He was gone. She loved him. She wanted him at her side, and yet… The wind around her blew hard and moaned through the rocks, giving voice to her silent grief. Her eyes hardened as she reached a decision. She no longer cared what everyone else said. Damn their judgements and proclamations. She would be with him. She would find a way. Someday, somehow, they would be together. She turned away from that spot and strode up the dunes towards the village, towards her father, towards her future. She was ready for action. Curses for all those who might stand in her way. She was through being told what to do.

The End

About the Author

Alisse Lee Goldenberg holds a Bachelor of Education and a fine arts degree; she has studied fantasy and folklore since she was a child. Alisse lives in Toronto, Canada, with her husband, Brian, and their triplets Joseph, Phillip, and Hailey. This is her second book in The Children of Colondona Series and she is also the author of the *Sitnalta Series*, *The Dybbuk Scrolls Trilogy*, as well as the *Bath Salts Series*, which is co-authored by An Tran. Please feel free to visit her at **www.alisseleegoldenberg.com**.

Thank you for purchasing this copy of **The Island of Mystics,** the second book in **The Children of Colonodona Series**. If you enjoyed this book, please let the author know by posting a review.

pandamoon
publishing

Growing good ideas into great reads...one book at a time.

Visit www.pandamoonpublishing.com to learn more about other works by our talented authors.

Mystery/Thriller/Suspense

- *A Flash of Red* by Sarah K. Stephens
- *Evening in the Yellow Wood* by Laura Kemp
- *Fate's Past* by Jason Huebinger
- *Graffiti Creek* by Matt Coleman
- *Juggling Kittens* by Matt Coleman
- *Killer Secrets* by Sherrie Orvik
- *Knights of the Shield* by Jeff Messick
- *Kricket* by Penni Jones
- *Looking into the Sun* by Todd Tavolazzi
- *On the Bricks Series Book 1: On the Bricks* by Penni Jones
- *Rogue Saga Series Book 1: Rogue Alliance* by Michelle Bellon
- *Southbound* by Jason Beem
- *The Juliet* by Laura Ellen Scott
- *The Last Detective* by Brian Cohn
- *The Moses Winter Mysteries Book 1: Made Safe* by Francis Sparks
- *The New Royal Mysteries Book 1: The Mean Bone in Her Body* by Laura Ellen Scott
- *The New Royal Mysteries Book 2: Crybaby Lane* by Laura Ellen Scott
- *The Ramadan Drummer* by Randolph Splitter
- *The Teratologist* by Ward Parker
- *The Unraveling of Brendan Meeks* by Brian Cohn
- *The Zeke Adams Series Book 1: Pariah* by Ward Parker
- *This Darkness Got to Give* by Dave Housley

Science Fiction/Fantasy

- *Becoming Thuperman* by Elgon Williams
- *Children of Colondona Book 1: The Wizard's Apprentice* by Alisse Lee Goldenberg
- *Children of Colondona Book 2: The Island of Mystics* by Alisse Lee Goldenberg
- *Chimera Catalyst* by Susan Kuchinskas
- *Dybbuk Scrolls Trilogy Book 1: The Song of Hadariah* by Alisse Lee Goldenberg
- *Dybbuk Scrolls Trilogy Book 2: The Song of Vengeance* by Alisse Lee Goldenberg
- *Dybbuk Scrolls Trilogy Book 3: The Song of War* by Alisse Lee Goldenberg
- *Everly Series Book 1: Everly* by Meg Bonney
- *.EXE Chronicles Book 1: Hello World* by Alexandra Tauber and Tiffany Rose
- *Fried Windows (In a Light White Sauce)* by Elgon Williams
- *Magehunter Saga Book 1: Magehunter* by Jeff Messick
- *Project 137* by Seth Augenstein
- *Revengers Series Book 1: Revengers* by David Valdes Greenwood
- *The Bath Salts Journals: Volume One* by Alisse Lee Goldenberg and An Tran
- *The Crimson Chronicles Book 1: Crimson Forest* by Christine Gabriel
- *The Crimson Chronicles Book 2: Crimson Moon* by Christine Gabriel
- *The Phaethon Series Book 1: Phaethon* by Rachel Sharp
- *The Sitnalta Series Book 1: Sitnalta* by Alisse Lee Goldenberg
- *The Sitnalta Series Book 2: The Kingdom Thief* by Alisse Lee Goldenberg
- *The Sitnalta Series Book 3: The City of Arches* by Alisse Lee Goldenberg
- *The Sitnalta Series Book 4: The Hedgewitch's Charm* by Alisse Lee Goldenberg
- *The Sitnalta Series Book 5: The False Princess* by Alisse Lee Goldenberg
- *The Wolfcat Chronicles Book 1: Wolfcat 1* by Elgon Williams

Women's Fiction

- *Beautiful Secret* by Dana Faletti
- *The Long Way Home* by Regina West
- *The Mason Siblings Series Book 1: Love's Misadventure* by Cheri Champagne
- *The Mason Siblings Series Book 2: The Trouble with Love* by Cheri Champagne
- *The Mason Siblings Series Book 3: Love and Deceit* by Cheri Champagne
- *The Mason Siblings Series Book 4: Final Battle for Love* by Cheri Champagne
- *The Seductive Spies Series Book 1: The Thespian Spy* by Cheri Champagne
- *The Seductive Spy Series Book 2: The Seamstress and the Spy* by Cheri Champagne
- *The Shape of the Atmosphere* by Jessica Dainty
- *The To-Hell-And-Back Club Book 1: The To-Hell-And-Back Club* by Jill Hannah Anderson
- *The To-Hell-And-Back Club Book 2: Crazy Little Town Called Love* by Jill Hannah Anderson